Also by R.D. Skillings

Alternative Lives (Ithaca House) 1974

Apple-wood Press • Cambridge/Newton • 1980

ACKNOWLEDGMENTS

"Dade City," "The Life," "North Cambridge," "Image," appeared in *Statements: New Fiction from the Fiction Collective* (George Braziller).

"Priorities," "Bravery," "See," "Dreams of Italian Hairdresser," appeared in *Statements 2* (George Braziller)

"Space," "Nice," "Thanksgiving," appeared in *Rapport 4* (Slow Lorris Press).

"On the Table," "Boom," "College," "Tall," "?," "Drunk," "Why," "Stupid Baby," "Sweet Necessity," "My Uncle Joe," "Worms in the A&P," "The Ultimate Question," appeared in *Provincetown Poets.*

Many of the stories in P-town Stories first appeared in *Shankpainter.*

ISBN: 0-918222-14-1 hardcover
ISBN: 0-918222-15-X paperback

Some of the places and institutions mentioned in this book do exist. The people of *P-town Stories* are not real. Any resemblance to persons living or dead is unintentional and coincidental.

 For information write to the Apple-wood Press, Box 2870, Cambridge, Massachusetts 02139.

P-town Stories

For Barbara Baker

CONTENTS

Summer

Fall

Winter

Spring

Summer

HOME

Provincetown aspires to the condition of Venice. It'll never make it, except maybe in smells. Coming down Ciro's white-shelled alley on a hot murky night you get the luxuriant gardens, roses and honeysuckle, then a tinge of rotting garbage, then a whiff of skunk and finally — back of that, subtler, pervasive, for a stiffening instant unrecognizably nostalgic — the cesspools. Then your breath blows it away and you go on to your pleasures, oblivious to the pitted finger of land lapped by the treacherous sea.

14

THE STREET

You know them both but sometimes it's years before you attach the name to the face. That's the nature of the place, there's this one long narrow street from end to end along the bay and everybody uses it, it's a small town underneath the summer mob. You become visible again when the tourists leave.

You're standing beside your neighbor in line at the A&P and you don't speak, you see plenty of him, you have nothing to say, but anybody from outside seeing you wouldn't even know you knew each other. You act like perfect strangers half the time. I mean you can't say hello to everyone, it would be absurd. Hello, lo, lo, lo, lo. You couldn't survive.

There's a whole unique etiquette of greeting evolved here, degrees of recognition. Say you're walking and you meet someone in a car, he might raise one finger on the wheel and hardly look at you or two fingers after he's known you a while or all four fingers for a friend or all the fingers on both hands or both hands off the wheel and a big grin, depending on your relations at the moment and his state of mind. Sometimes you're stuck at the first finger for years. Of course either or both can always adopt the preoccupied blind stare.

That's simple compared to meetings on foot. You might just drop your eyes or smile or you might nod or open your mouth and raise your eyebrows or actually speak or stop and really get into it. The weather's usually worth a few words, it changes about three times a day.

Personally I can always tell if I've got my act together by whether I can face all the eyes on the meatrack. That's the row of green benches in front of Town Hall. In daylight it's a little like the bleachers, at night it's a sort of hotel lobby. When I get too high I'm tempted to take the beach around or go by Back Street.

Say you have a subsequent experience with someone you've been nodding to for years, after that you always say hello. It might stay there for years but things can dwindle too. If nothing else happens you lapse from speaking and just nod, then you stop nodding, then you stop with the eyes and finally you forget how it started or even that you ever knew each other.

One thing's sure though. You can stay here forever but you'll never be a native if you're not.

SPACE

for Michael Casey

It was this beautiful day, I was on my way to the Fo'c's'le, I can't stand the sun you know and out comes Mr. Nelson, I work for him sometimes, and says You won't believe what just happened to me. He was all indignant because he found a dead seagull on the beach in front of his house so he called the Sanitation Department and told them to come over and get it and they said you know Take care of it yourself, everybody has to do his share, but he said you know That's their business.

Well get a shovel I said You can bury it yourself. Oh I don't think I could handle that he said. It isn't heavy I said The sand isn't hard. Oh I can't handle that he said. So I did it for him and he gave me five dollars. Next day the tide dug it up again. Must've spaced him out.

17

NARK

Did I tell you about my Nark?

Saturday afternoon I was sitting in the Surf Club with my cribbage board so this guy comes over and I said to myself This guy must be a Nark, what else could he be? He's got this little porkpie hat and short hair and a beerbelly and he drives a buggy with you know slogans painted all over it like MAKE LOVE NOT WAR and he's very uptight, so we played 15 games of cribbage, he's not bad, we split about even, and I figure Well he's trying to make me. All the time he's drinking Canadian Club. He's got his wife stashed in a motel in Truro and his brother's wife spots us in the window and he's all embarrassed to be seen with me. He and his brother had said they were going fishing.

Well he's not a bad guy except he's so jumpy so I say Come on home for dinner. I don't know what he thought he was getting into but he came. All the kids were there and about forty other people so I made some dinner and after that we started playing cribbage again, he's hooked on cribbage, all the while he's drinking Canadian Club and having the time of his life.

Everybody figured he was a little weird but nobody said anything and all of a sudden he says You're being too nice to me, why're you all being so nice? and bursts out sobbing and starts telling us what a rotten guy he is, how he fucks girls and then busts them and keeps the dope. He got transferred down here from Boston because they sent him to spy on some meeting of college radicals and there was a bottle of Canadian Club there and he got drunk and fell asleep and they suspended him for four months without pay.

He kept asking us how much we paid an ounce you know because he gets it for free, and I kept saying I never bought it, people just laid it on me, and he kept talking about this good acid he got off a guy and how he'd give us some, there was getting to be a little menace in all this, you know how some guys'll try to make you by intimidation.

Well it's getting later and later, it's after midnight and he keeps saying he's got to go home, he's throwing his car keys up in the air and catching them like a little kid and can you imagine? he drops them through a crack in the sundeck, it had to be unconscious, and of course it's high tide so I say I'll drive you home and you can get the keys in the morning and he says Okay if you'll come in when we get there and explain to my wife. I said I would not and he wound up sleeping on the couch.

NICE

My boyfriend? The last one? The one that looked like a criminal? Oh he left town, he had to get out, he couldn't take it any more, he's on vacation. I don't even want to think about him. He got to beating me up. One time he sat on my chest with his knees on my arms and hit me, it didn't matter what I said, Yes or No, he'd still hit me. He'd ask me these weird questions and then he'd hit me. I think he just liked hitting me, I don't even want to think about that. I had two black eyes. He was a real bastard, he was nice though.

VINNIE

Vinnie and I split up yesterday. I came home, there were about six people there smoking and this bitch was sitting on his lap. I didn't say anything you know I came in with Don, at least I don't get caught. After a while two of the guys asked him if they could take me into town and he said all right, but I came right back. He wasn't expecting me so soon, he was upstairs fucking this bitch. On my side of the bed, on my pillow, everything! Don't worry about it he said. I won't I said and walked out the door and I haven't seen the bastard since.

20

WIFE

I was coming home from a party one night, it must've been three o'clock in the morning and I heard this car drive up beside me. I knew it was some creep, I didn't even look. He kept following me, he drove right up to the sidewalk. It was a red VW, guess who it was, it was Bob Barger, who else? He didn't recognize me. He leaned across the seat and rolled down the window and he said Chickadee shall we go to your place or mine? I put my head in the window, I said Bob are you kidding me? You should've seen his face.

I ran into him about a week later in the Fo'c's'le. He was very polite, very nervous, he kept buying me drinks. He never bought anybody a drink in his life, I was just sitting there getting high. Finally after we had about five drinks he said I hope you weren't offended that night, I was drunk, I didn't mean anything, I hope you won't mention it to anyone. I said Bob who would I mention it to? I guess he meant his wife.

AC/DC

I've been having an affair with this guy I used to know in New York, I hadn't seen him in a long time and then he turned up here for the summer. Anyway we got together again but one night we had a terrible scene in bed. I couldn't tell what he wanted, we were both drunk, he kept muttering You can't do me any good, you can't do a thing for me, and all of a sudden he got up and left. I felt awful, I thought maybe I'd been crude in some way, I felt as if I'd driven him away, and I went over to his place, I was going to apologize, and found him screwing his roommate, they're waiters in the same restaurant. I never knew he was gay, he always played the big stud with me. I know everybody's doing the AC/DC thing but I can't resign myself, I despise him now, I can't even talk to him. I keep thinking he should've told me.

BOOM

They got me up against the car and I said Boom-Boom-Boom and they said Boom-Boom-Boom. This is a church key I said This is a classic case not of police brutality but police stupidity. That was it man. They got me in handcuffs, I got charged with possession of a deadly weapon, drunk and disorderly, resisting arrest and using abusive language to a police officer. All over a parking ticket.

COLLEGE

When I was 16 or 17 I used to drink in a bar like this, I'd wait till my parents went to bed and then climb out the window. One night my father caught me coming in and he just picked up my stereo and threw it at the wall. That was when I decided I'd better go to college, get the hell out.

APOLOGIES TO THE ASTROLOGERS

Randall Rowan fucked five different chicks on five nights in a row last summer. They never crossed, they never bumped, not one came back, he's got them under control. I don't know how he does it, I used to watch them going up the stairs. He's a Virgo, very logical and correct, when he goes away he leaves Lysol in the toilet, I don't know why we get along so well, I'm a Taurus, we argue, he always winds up saying Feeling, what good's that?

They were all young and beautiful. One of them though was loud, the walls are thin, he put on a record to cover her up, I could hear her saying Aw don't hand me that bullshit, I don't want to hear any of that bullshit. He probably had to fucker to shuter up. I can just see Randall up there, he must've been mortified, he hates any breach of decorum.

EMBARRASSMENT

I'm so embarrassed. I O.D.'d the other night and wound up in jail. I went to this party, I got there late, there was acid in the punch but nobody told me, there was none left anyway. I went around finishing up all the cups on the sills, you know what a drunk I am. I had a nice high till I freaked out. All of a sudden my head was empty, there was nothing in there, so I got on my bicycle to go to Piggy's, I got halfway there and I jumped off, I was really freaking out, I scratched my knees and cut my face, I was awful, I was lying there in the bushes trying to figure out what happened. My god the cops were right behind me. They got out of the car and picked me up. I thought they must've beat me up, I began to scream at them, I called them Nazis, I tried to bite their wrists. They took me down to the station, I said I was going to sue them for false arrest, they wouldn't let me go until I signed something, I said I'm not signing anything. They got the Police Matron, I kept shouting at her Don't you touch me you fucking cunt. Next morning I woke up in jail. I'm so embarrassed.

TALL

I was standing in line at the A&P, there was a woman behind me, she said When I was a girl they said I was tall but look at you, you're taller than I am, you must be six feet. I could hardly digest that, I didn't know what to say, I just turned around. She said Oh you're not a girl, she was very upset. I said It must've been the mustache that fooled you, and she changed lines.

24

DRUNK

We picked up a drunk last night on the way to The Hermit. He was disgusting, he was slobbering in the gutter, I don't know why we brought him along, we were bored, we thought he'd entertain us. He was obnoxious to everyone, he insulted the waitress, he spilled his coffee on me, then he put the make on Mark. Finally he knocked the table over, he was very pleased with himself.

FAME

Terry Southern was here part of one summer, he was wined and dined around, he wound up staying at Phil's, he was everybody's honored guest but he'd say these embarrassingly cloddish things and we'd all think God how could this be? Then someone showed up who knew Southern. Nobody wanted to expose the guy, the comedy went on quite a while. Finally I said Don't worry about it but everybody knows you're not Terry Southern. He says Don't bug me man just don't bug me. Next day he disappeared with Phil's I.D. cards and we never saw him again.

25

MY BOUT WITH MIDDLE AMERICA

I was takin LSD about once a week. I was goin with this 21 year old black kid, we had a thing, I still don't know what it was, pickin fleas off each other, we were very intimate.

I had a vaginal infection not clap that didn't get cured. A doctor in Boston diagnosed it and treated it and said it was all gone.

So one weekend, I wanted to be alone with Willie, we were goin to take acid, these friends arrived. I was very aggravated, that was back in the days when I kept my mouth shut, now I tell people. I said What're you doin here? They said We thought we'd take acid with you. I said Where you goin to get the acid? They said We thought you'd give us some.

So, you know. We sat around and looked at the ocean, I got off pretty good. I began to have these pains in my stomach, by midnight I was doubled up on the floor. I called Tower and said Prescribe me something. He said Take some paragoric. I thought you know it'll be gone in the morning, tomorrow's a new day.

Next morning it's still there so I filled myself full of codeine, killed the pain, I was very stoned, very dopey, I didn't know what was goin on. Next day the pain's up in my shoulders, you know I'm beginning to get worried, so I went to A.I.M. and the doctor took a blood test. He said You've got a 40,000 white count instead of 5,000, I can't treat you, you'd better go to Hyannis Hospital. I said Uh-uh. He said You'll be in a box by tomorrow if you don't, and he gave me this piece of paper with my blood count on it.

So I went home and called Diane. She says Take an enema. By this time I'm blowing up like a balloon, every time I ate something I'd just swell, my stomach was like a fireball. Diane says D'you want me to drive you to the hospital? Never mind I said I'll drive, it's not that important.

Next day I drove to Hyannis, I'm really high on codeine and I'm still on the tailend of this acid trip, Willie's sittin there beside me. He's got shades and long corkscrew hair, he's beboppin, jivin you know crazy, and all the way he's drawin stuff out the window with a Rapidograph.

When we got there they never would've let us in except I had this piece of paper that said my white count was 40,000. Right away I could see we had a racial problem. They were horrified by Willie, we were sittin there in the waitin room, he's so nervous he's drawin pictures of the pipes, the washbowl, his shoes, everything. They hate you you know. I was this 40 year old Miss Hippie, Miss Beatnik you know long hair and beads, all their worst fantasies. If I'd been a black woman it wouldn't've been so bad.

I got Dr. Fawley, that's Ann's doctor, he's stern, she digs him, she needs a father figure, he's real murder, he starts asking me questions about drugs. He sent Willie home, I'm lyin there in pain. I told him about the codeine and paregoric. He kept sayin What else, what else? Finally he got it out of me. I said I'd had some acid three days ago, a little bit. He railed at me. Makes you feel good huh? Makes you happy huh? He worked me over about drugs, he had this unbelievable contempt.

So then he stuck an intravenous needle in my arm with this you know bottle slung in a rack and rammed a tube in my nose and down the back of my throat, he wasn't a bit gentle. Next thing I know there's an intern tryin to get me to sign this paper releasin them to operate. I wouldn't sign. The nurse is pushin the bed down the hallway and this guy's wavin this paper in my face tryin to get me to sign it. In the operatin room I kept sittin up. I said You're not cuttin anything outa me, and the surgeon says to the anesthesiologist Haven't you got her down yet?

I had peritonitis and an obstruction of the intestine from the infection. They never should've operated, they could've tried antibiotics first.

Willie came boppin in next day expectin to see me all

better, ready to go home and dance. They ran him through the wringer. I'm sorry he had to go through that thing alone, I was almost out, I was just lyin there, I couldn't function.

They kept me incommunicado five days. I couldn't even make a phone call. I told Willie to call Diane but he didn't. I was in this private room, I was a prisoner, they wouldn't bring a phone in. They said You can make a call when you're on your feet.

The nurse hated me, it used to freak her out, Willie and I'd be neckin. She tried to starve me, she'd rip the tape off my arm like she was checkin to make sure the needle was in, she'd leave it out till the doctor came around the next day, I lost 15 pounds. One time when she gave me my ration of morphine I let out this big sigh of relief. Willie says Don't do that, they'll think you're a junkie.

So the doctor comes around again. He says You got the clap. That's the word he used. You know what it means to them, orgies, blacks, longhairs, like their daughters aren't gettin it, they better watch out for their wives. I said No I don't have the clap, it was diagnosed up in Boston. He says Oh yes you do kiddo, you got the clap. He gave me a whole moral lecture, I'm lyin there with this tube in my nose. There's not much you can do except keep away from the bastards, they'll kill you if they can.

28

WORMS IN THE A&P

All I wanted was some razor blades, the place was mobbed, the pushcarts were snarled, this guy says to me, he's standing around waiting for his wife, Don't buy those, buy this other kind. He gives me a consumer report on the best buy in razor blades, this one's adjustable, that one's not, you get 6 for 79¢ with this one, 8 for 83¢ with that, he was trying to be helpful I'm sure.

I started shouting at him Who cares? What difference does it make? You think it matters? Everyone was staring at us, he looked away like I was some kind of a lunatic, he looked hurt actually.

I got in line and these two women were saying how terrible the crowds were. The lines were moving about an inch an hour and they were all a mile long. They were really indignant, I got mad all over again. I said How about suicide as an alternative? They said No. You're very definite about that I said and they both turned away like I was a worm.

MY UNCLE JOE

for Saphira

He's my favorite of all my family. He had a little farm down in North Carolina where all my people came from, he was coming home one day, it was the Depression and he found this starving horse lying in a field. It was so thin the bones were sticking through, the buzzards were circling around.

He got the horse home in his truck and he force-fed it a mixture of something and something and baking soda. Pretty soon it began to blossom, it swelled up nice and fat and sleek and it began to walk around and Uncle Joe sold it to his neighbor for $100.

The first day the neighbor was out plowing behind the horse it broke this enormous wind and fell down dead, it was like all the air going out of a balloon, like it zigzagged across the field, it shriveled down to nothing. The neighbor didn't think too much of Uncle Joe after that, he was a real con man.

MUGGED

I got mugged crossing Cambridge Common one night. Five young blacks surrounded me and began going through my pockets. It was about a week after those two twelve-year old kids were killed in Roxbury trying to rob a grocery store, I only had 35¢ on me, I began to lecture them, I said you know You'll get in trouble doing this kind of thing. They gathered all my pennies and nickles and dimes and ran off, but there was one older one, he stayed around and I started talking to him. I said This is not good, you shouldn't lead them this way, they'll end up getting shot. I think he agreed with me, we got along all right and after a while he wanted to shake hands with me. Listen I said I'm not shaking hands with you, you're not my friend, you've got my money. So he called the kids back and made them give me back my 35¢ and then we all shook hands and I went home.

31

SWEET NECESSITY

Paula had been on the meatrack since morning, strungout, hungry and hungover. Her shoes and bathing suit were rolled up in her jacket under the bench and her anxious eyes searched the passing mob.

In three days she'd never got to the beach once, though that was why she'd come. She could see a little bit of the bay glittering between the shops across the street, like a piece of a picture puzzle, white sand and blue sea with bathers, fifty yards away, but she couldn't leave the meatrack.

The speed freak limped by again and she looked away. "How you doin?" he'd shouted once when she'd met his eyes. Face burned red, bare feet blistered, he'd been walking the street all day, up and down, like an angry scarecrow, going past in opposite directions every 20 minutes, and finally he'd become aware of her always there watching him, while the other inhabitants of the benches changed with the hours. He hated the sight of her and she knew it.

Billy Birdman came strolling. "Where'd you disappear to?" he said.

"You seen Alma? She's supposed to meet me here."

"I haven't seen anybody, I just got up," said Billy "What did you leave for?"

"I've got to get back to New York," she said. "Alma's got my bus fare, I gave it to her so I wouldn't drink it."

"She probably drank it," Billy said.

"She can't," Paula said, "she took some pills that'll make her sick. She took so many she probably got off on them."

"The last bus goes at six," said Billy.

"Then I'll have to hitch," she said.

"It's going to rain," Billy said, cocking his eye at the black sky. A wind was coming up.

Paula bared her dry teeth in a bitter smile. What had she ever learned, except she was doomed to repeat? Three days she'd lived in the bars, crashing on floors or in cars, and eating crap. She'd meant to walk the beach alone, swim and embrace her soul, but the minute they arrived they met some guys with mescaline and then it was a continuous trance of parties and pills and confused migrations from place to place. She couldn't remember where she'd met Billy, only that he'd sat by the bed for hours, rubbing her belly.

"Come," he said, "I'll buy you a slice of pizza."

"Will you bring me one?"

"I'm not coming back this way. How come you left, you don't like balling me?"

"Sure," she said. "Why not?"

"Then come on," he said, jerking his head. "I know somebody who's got dynamite dope."

"I've got to get back to New York."

"No you don't," he said, his black eyes darting everywhere in the summer crowd, "you don't have to do anything, you can stay here, you can go to New York, you can do whatever."

"I'm on methadone," she explained in exasperation, "if I don't get back soon I'm going to be very sick."

Billy did a deft little soft-shoe two-step with his head on one side. "Then I guess you'll go," he said and walked off.

"Give me a cigarette at least," she called but he didn't stop.

From the other direction four cops moving so fast and smooth they might've been on wheels hustled down the block each carrying a limb of the speed freak who kept shouting, "You're liars, you killed him, not me."

The clot of struggle swirled along the walk and disappeared down the basement steps under the Town Hall. The pennants on the roof of the outdoor cafe where tourists were drinking ices snapped in the rising wind and the first drops fell.

In terror Paula grabbed her bundle and ran for the bus, praying Alma would be there. Where was she, her oldest friend? Between the shops laughing streams of people were coming off the beach. Paula had a momentary vision of Alma drowning, eyes wide and blind, seaweed in her hair, and knew when the bus left she would start for the highway without a search.

DEMOGRAPHY

Two straight college guys
sitting on the meatrack
amazed at the gays going by
began counting them
on a matchbook cover 𝍸.
They got to a dozen, no end
in sight. There's another!
Look at that one! Look at him!

I wanted to say And them darling
and them and them and all of them.
They were only getting the queens
of course.

THE MEATRACK

I used to sit on the benches every day before the Selectmen took them away, they had to, there're so many hippies. The benches are for the townspeople not pigs like them, they leave their filth underneath, they commit sex crimes at night, they burn incense inside our law-abiding town hall, they smell, don't ever sit downwind, they look awful, they have no pride, some of them come from good families too. I don't mind long hair on girls.

Well look at Sally Souza! Who does she think she is? She can hardly fit inside those pants. Wait till her mother finds out, I'm not going to be the one to tell her. I wish there was some place to sit down, coffee costs a quarter everywhere now, I won't pay that. It's a sad day for this town when they have to take the benches away.

YES

On weekends
we always wanted
to get up early
in order to have lots of time
to do something but we could never
seem to finish making love
before noon and breakfast
wasn't done until one,
though it wasn't a bad life,
all in all.

AT SARA'S

Beet greens from the garden, pan-fried potatoes and browned round onions, summer squash on a bed of boiled cabbage, sliced tomatoes in vinegar sprinkled with parsley, garlic bread spiked with hot peppers, smoked shoulder, Scotch, wine and milk.

DRY

I can always tell when it's August, the tourists go crazy. I got to the bookstore oh about ten after ten and there were some people waiting. I unlocked the door and went in for a second to get some money, I came right out, they were pushing to get in, I literally had to push to keep them out. I said I'm going to get a cup of coffee, I'll be right back. They were mad as hops, they followed me down the street asking if I had this, if I had that, and I said to myself It must be August. They couldn't wait to buy a book, it wasn't even raining.

SHAPE OF THE YEAR

This is my month to be groovy, if I'm not groovy in August I'm never going to be, I'll have to wait another year. Everybody's about to go home, the girls are getting riper by the minute. Too bad they never fall in my lap, I'm ready and willing, I'm here with open arms, I'm just not groovy I guess. By fall everybody's found somebody for the winter. You've got to be groovy though. How d'you like my new shoes, pretty snazzy eh? You don't see many of these around, 79¢, that's 39½¢ apiece. I'm fair game for the foot fetishists. That's no joke either. I knew a girl who fell in love with a pair of boots, not mine I should say at the outset of this unfortunate and typical anecdote. I invited her to dinner, I don't feel so bad, we went Dutch, she saw some boots under the next table, she said I've got to find out who this guy is, she moved her meal over, she said I hope you don't mind. Go ahead I said and she went off with him, story of my life. You seen Alba lately, she looks almost good enough to be eating material.

38

MORTAL MEN

Some people you never associate with death, you can't imagine it, it seems they're part of life, they'll go on forever and no troubles, but they're mortal men like everybody. I was surprised when Dr. Tower died, he brought half the people in this town into the world. He was rich, he had two pages of property in the annual list. You'd always see him driving that big car, one night he had a heart attack on a house call, he was 90 years old.

Then there was Sal Silva. He had the best boat, he went out in all weather. He wore a blue velvet cap and a big silver buckle, all the women loved him, I don't say he didn't have troubles. After he was seized, he was lying in bed, all his relatives was gathered round, he sat up and said I don't want to die, I ain't going to die, I don't want to die, I ain't going to die, and fell back dead.

Then there was Paully Noons, he was the mortician, he put away a lot of people, think of the thousands. You'd hear so and so'd died and you'd know Paully Noons would be up there on the hill taking care of him, he must've got to feeling invincible. He always had a joke and he'd always loan you two bucks for a bottle.

So one day word comes down that Paully Noons is dead. I couldn't believe it, I said Paully Noons? They says Yes, that's right. That's right. When the time comes for you to go you've got to go whether you want to go or not, whoever you are, no two ways about it.

PIGGY'S

Look at the corruption in the faces, all that wonderful anarchy. It's a good place for art, you'll have time to develop, people live a long time here and do as they please. Take that gnome over there with white hair, he's the most dissipated person I know, it's a way of life with him, he works every day and improves, he's a closet painter actually, nothing distracts him, he's 25, he looks 50, he's a complete degenerate, he's an ice-cold clam in the mud here.

BATTLE OF THE BULGE

Betty Beverly's husband
won the Medal of Honor
and $400 a month
over his ordinary pension
for killing 11 Germans
with a knife,
coming up behind them in the fog,
then machine-gunning their command post.
He said everybody liked him
because he didn't smoke
and gave away his cigarettes.
Modest, he never talked about it,
sat home all day drinking beer
and finally became such a wreck
he went to the VA Hospital
where they dried him out. Now
he doesn't drink or do anything.

41

BRAVERY

You hear how bad it is in New York, you hear how bad it is in St. Thomas, it's worse right in my own back yard. This guy came right into my house. I was just sitting down to dinner, I had daffodils on the table. I'm a married woman I said I just got done watching my husband die four months, what d'you want with me? He grabbed my arm and dragged me from room to room. I've had my eye on you for years he said. Well you must need glasses I said I'm an old woman. I looked better than I do now, at least I had my hair up. He kept coming back, he terrorized me a whole month. He lives right in town here, he's got a black beard. I went to the police but they said they couldn't do anything unless I signed a warrant, they wouldn't even go talk to him. He's a married man, he's got kids, I didn't want to get him in trouble. I met him on the street one day, I saw him coming, I didn't know what to do, run or what, but I was mad, I went right up to him, I looked him right in the eye and I said I'm not trembling, I'm not shaking, I'm not even afraid of you, but if you're going to make trouble for me in a public place you'll be sorry, I'll see to it, that's a promise. You know what he said? He said No hard feelings? I said No and he never bothered me again. Was I brave or what? You got to stand up to the bastards.

42

WATER BED

I don't like to do it, it's my wife's idea, I hate to evict anyone, it's not a pleasant thing to have to do. They're nice people no doubt but they're into some things that don't add up. I'll admit they've always paid the rent on time but with four of them they're getting the place cheap. We've never had more than three people in that unit, I'd be justified in raising them $100 a month. As a matter of fact they've had a very reasonable deal. I don't know where their money comes from, they always pay in small bills, maybe they're using drugs down there, I don't want any trouble with the police. One of them was in jail once, I happen to know. I've got some prospective tenants, very reliable people, mature working people, they won't just take off on me in the middle of the night, I can't afford any risks, I've got mortgage payments to meet.

I hate to do it but Sally insists and maybe she's right. For myself I don't care what their living situation is, it's none of my business what they do. All the same it doesn't look well, I mean you don't know who's doing what with who, heh-heh. I don't want the neighbors to think I'm running a bordello, I don't want them annoying my other tenants, I have a responsibility to them.

I don't mind long hair and eccentric dress, I don't care what their sexual proclivities are but there's got to be a limit, there's just too many, two men and a woman and a baby and that mangy dog, he growled at me one day, they weren't home, I almost kicked him. I went in and looked around, the place stank of incense, it wasn't dirty, it could've been cleaner, I've got no complaints about that.

Then they put a waterbed in there without asking my

permission. They all sleep on it, all four of them, it's too heavy for that floor, those are old floors. There's no reason I should have to put up with that shit. They don't have a lease, I have a perfect legal right. I hate to be a bastard but it's their own fault, I guess they'll find someplace else.

44

HIGH CONSTRUCTION

I got a pin in my elbow, I got a pin in my knee. I lost seven months. Luckily I wasn't up very high. I knew a guy, he was six-three, you know a man's instinct is to land on his feet, when they scraped him up he was about four feet tall, it drives your hip bones up to your armpits.

I'm doin pretty well when you consider, I'm pullin down $32,000 a year. I didn't have no father, Ma brought up the six of us, we were always poor, we never had enough to eat. I went in the Marines when I was 18, I didn't even finish high school. I been in 32 countries, 33 counting Canada, and 24 states, I bummed around a lot when I got out. I was married a year, I got a kid, costs me $100 a month in support.

I ran into Sal Cornish the other day. He's an accountant, he had five years of college, I couldn't help tellin him how much I was makin, I think he was a little bit resentful, you know because of all that education. He used to be too good to talk to people like me, Gilly Watts turned out okay too. He's a teller down in the Savings and Loan, I went in there the day I got back, I said I want to open an account. That was two years ago, I never put another cent in, I just wanted him to know who I was. He said For how much? I put down $2000, four $500 bills, I liked seeing his eyes bug out. He's got fat. I'm pretty solid, I'm hard as a rock, you gotta be in my business. Look at these hands, these ain't no banker's hands. I got about $350 in my wallet right now.

I learned how to handle myself in the Marines, I've got a Black Belt. I put four guys in the hospital one night, I earned a lot of respect that way I wouldn't have got otherwise. I don't fight much any more, I don't have to, I got a reputation. If I can walk away from it I will, I don't take no shit though, I don't let it look like I'm afraid.

I'm thirty, I've got another four-five years, six at most. It's a young man's game, your reflexes go. Sometimes up there in winter the wind's so cold in your face it makes the tears come. You're up eight-ten stories, you're on a six inch beam, one mistake, one wrong step they'll be calling you Shorty. That's why I don't make too many plans. My uncle, he never did nothin, he dropped dead at 42, so who knows?

Last year I bought an apartment house, I fixed it up myself working weekends. I figure if I can get two more I'll retire and live on the income. I got a new car, I got two boats, I got a duck blind, I got guns, I didn't get to go huntin once this year, I used to go all the time.

It's nice to see you again. How you doin? I'd consider it a privilege, I'd appreciate it if you'd let me buy you a drink. Bartender, Chivas Regal. Doubles.

46

PUT-ON

I was a stewardess on Overseas Airways, this rickety DC6 with a top speed of about 110, you'd open a window when you wanted to cool off. One time I went into the cockpit and there was a pair of gloves on the wheel and nobody there. I went all over the plane looking for the pilot and co-pilot. I looked in the bathroom, I looked in the tail, I looked at all the passengers. They were calm, they didn't know the plane was being flown by this pair of gloves, there wasn't much traffic in those days between Guam and Wake. I couldn't figure it out, I was panicked, I thought I'm going to have to land this thing myself. It turned out there was a little hatch leading to the landing gear big enough for two men to squeeze in. They were just putting me on.

47

DAYS IN THE LIFE

Some people don't think a bartender can hear, he's like a hat rack. One of the worst arguments I ever had to listen to was between this couple who used to come every night, an older man and a young woman. They went on for about an hour and a half like they were in their own living room, they didn't even lower their voices. The last thing she said was I don't give a shit what you say, I still think I'm salvageable.

I said to Dee Dee, she was the waitress, Did you hear that? She said Yes. I said Would you like to take a walk? She said I'd love to. So I climbed over the bar and she took off her apron and we went out for a walk, arm-in-arm, strolling down the street, for about 15 minutes, there was a nice moon. I mean what do people think of themselves?

Another time, it was early in the evening, these two guys came in, one was a little rosy-cheeked guy with white hair and a tweed coat on, he looked like the Head Librarian from some little town in the midwest. He held his straw hat in his lap and he spoke with a thlight lithp. He said Bartender. I said Yes Sir? He said It's a good thing these stools are thoft, I've been fucked up the ass four times today and I'm very tender. The guy beside him was a muscular young bruiser in one of those see-through undershirts, I suppose he meant him.

Dee Dee said How would you like to take a walk? I said Absolutely and climbed over the bar and we went out for a walk. I have no objection you understand to what happened to him, what I mind is having it inflicted on us.

Another time, at the end of the night, I picked up an empty glass and there was a $20 bill under it and a little note all folded up that said I think you're cute, I'd like to suck you off, come to Room 21 at the Holiday Inn.

I don't even know who left it. I showed it to Dee Dee, I said What d'you say we split this? She nodded, I rang it up on the cash register, you know zero-zero, and I gave her ten and I took ten. I dropped the twenty in the drawer and we went home.

49

AIR POWER

I went over there with an open mind, I said you'd better see for yourself before you make a judgment. It didn't take long, we were burning villages and shooting people. My buddy got right into it, you have to to survive I guess. He was against the war when we first got there but he wound up gungho, we weren't even friends any more. Another guy got his limbs blown off, he was lying there looking right in my eyes and he said What're we doing here anyway? I couldn't say anything, you don't like to lie to a man who's dying.

Right after that mission I looked out the barracks window one morning and saw a jet coming, it was one of ours but for some reason I was sure it was a MIG. I thought we were going to get paid back in full for everything we'd done, I started screaming, I couldn't stop. The medics shot me full of dope, cooled me out. I don't think about it so much any more. Sometimes though it all comes back and then I see that MIG. I don't think you ever get over a thing like that.

WAY TO GO

There's a certain sort of guy,
he's hip, he comes equipped
with pot and pills and poppers—
amyl nitrate—which I detest.
He's a scientist of sex,
he has it all down pat,
he gives you this
and then it's time for that,
he doesn't even ask.
When you get breathing fast
he snaps it under your nose.
I thought I was going to die.

51

RIGHTS

There were about twenty of us there. Bill Oliver was the only one drinking, everyone else was tripping or stoned or something, and there was this knock on the door and the cops came in. There were about six pounds of dope on the table, the smoke was so thick you couldn't see three feet in front of you. They were stepping over stuff, trying to ignore everything. One of them coughed and said the neighbors had complained about the noise and would we keep it down please. Bill jumped up off the floor and said Where's your search warrant, you can't come in here without a search warrant, I know my rights. This poor cop kept coughing, he was all embarrassed. Luckily somebody shoveled Bill off to the bathroom and they left. We just turned the music down and continued. Of course it was a respectable neighborhood.

52

DADE CITY

You won't believe this fucking scene. I just went to the Police Station to get an application for a pistol permit because I think we should all be armed. The guy behind the desk says What d'you want a pistol for? I says Why can't I have a pistol, you got a pistol. He says I'm a policeman. It went on that way awhile. Well I says I saw a nice pistol in a window up in Orleans, I want to buy it, I want to do some target shooting out in the woods, I already got a rifle permit.

He said If we gave everybody a permit who wanted one it'd be Dade City here, where you from? I told him Havana, Cuba. He hits his forehead with his palm like in the Polack jokes and says You want to hijack a plane? No I says I want to start a revolution. He says Why don't you get on your motor scooter and ride south? Four years in Korea I says and I can't have a pistol permit?

The rest of them're watching NYPD on TV, New York Police Department. We couldn't interrupt that, the other guys kept waving at us to keep quiet. He says You don't have any need for a pistol. I says I want to do some target shooting, all the while I'm going plink plink plink with my finger like I'm sighting just a little to the side of his head. He says Here's an application, good luck. I says If I don't get it I'm going to take it to the Supreme Court.

53

SIX

You know what it's like to be six years old now? Lemme tell you. I was down in Connecticut to see my wife, my ex. She lives in an apartment complex you know swimming pools, playgrounds, all that. Across the way there's this big shopping plaza, they stay open till like midnight. We're out there in the middle of this square, there's nobody out but there's this police helicopter going around. So it comes down to about 100 feet and puts a spotlight on us. There I am holding my son's hand, he's six years old. You know what he says? He says Those bastards, they always fuck up. They're looking for criminals but we're not criminals. They always fuck up.

What're you going to say? Don't use dirty language? He's six years old but already he knows where it's at.

IMAGE

Sometimes I think I'm going to die without ever escaping that room. It had a couch that pulled out where they slept. There was a crib where my brother and I slept, there was a yellow light, a window and a kind of stuffed chair. My father used to sit me on his knee and tell me about the Mexican Revolution. He fought, he shot people, they tied the rich to the railroad tracks, then he moved to America because he was tired of fighting. My mother was a waitress and drank herself to death at 37.

A memory I shall never escape, a memory I have every day of my life, is of my mother screaming and my father bending her back with one hand in her hair until she was like an acrobat while he held the iron she had been ironing his shirts with an inch from her face. That image is there every time I go to bed with a man.

55

KEEP LAUGHING, HANG ON TO YOUR LIFE

Five nondescript drinkers sat one rainy midnight Sunday in the east window of the Fo'c's'le, and examined a tourist with sharp irony, all except Rose who couldn't wait to get him home.

Playboy had offered him a $30,000 job in the publicity department and he had come to P-town to think it over, had just arrived in fact on the four o'clock bus and here he still was, looser and looser, his decrepit suitcase under the table, the press coming out of his clothes. He had begun to sway somewhat on the bench and waggle his head and laugh to himself. "They published a story of mine once," he said, "fifteen years ago."

"I used to write but the only stories I knew got too painful," Philly said around his cheroot. He spread his arms out on the window ledge and squinted at the smoke. "I'm a whore. I write how-to books. I make my living at it. Albert here's a serious writer, he's an artist. Doin his best anyway."

Albert, who wrote little, finished less and found no publishers, glared bravely at the tourist.

The tourist regarded him. "Can you imagine how much I'd have to spend on clothes?" he said.

"You'd better get the hell out of here on the next bus," Wade said. "It may be too late already."

"This is no place for fools," Weymouth said. "Look at us."

Shabby, grey and full of holes compared to the tourist who resembled a Madison Avenue ad, they were all there by choice, had been there for years, like barnacles. To Rose he looked luscious with his worn tanned face full of subterfuges. She liked his laugh and his little boy amazement at his luck. He had been unemployed for a long time and was tired of last resorts. He would have a home again if he took the job, but he would have to entertain, he would have to stay sober. He could drink like a fish and still write.

"I think you should stay here and finish your novel," Rose said. "You'll never do it in New York."

"Oh-ho, he's got a novel!" Philly roared, louder and louder the more he drank.

"A novel!" Wade breathed and his Pan-like eyes lit up. "All Albert can write is picayune little shit."

Albert shook his head in amazement, having known the tourist's brother in college fifteen years before, an utterly different type, though they looked exactly alike.

"He doesn't think much of me," the tourist had admitted ungrudgingly. "He's good, he looks after the parents. I haven't been home in years."

"What's your book about?" Weymouth said.

"Everything," said the tourist, swaying toward Rose with a leer. She chortled and his grin got out of control again.

"And what else?" said Philly, drumming his fingers, running his eyes around the empty bar.

"I've got it with me," said the tourist, righting himself. He fumbled open the suitcase. Shirts, toilet articles, another suit, a city man's gear, tumbled out with a scrambled mass of papers scrawled around the edges and a warped notebook. He blearily inspected handfuls of the yellow foolscap, dropped them back, then stewed around in another part of the pile. The papers were mainly upside-down and when he tried to flip the whole thing slabs of pages slithered away. Albert bent to read a line but everything visible was smudged and mistyped, most discouraging. The tourist finally collated three pages, smoothed them out in the beery ashes on the table and thrust them at Philly.

"I'll read it," Philly yelled doubtfully, between warning and good will, "I'll read it, you want me to read it?"

The tourist mutely left his hand outstretched, ducked under the table again, repacking his possessions.

" All right," Philly said in the tones of a disclaimer, took the pages and straightened his glasses, plucked at his beard. Albert, preparing to cringe, huddled forward fetally, closed one eye, turned the other out the window. On the edge of sleep Weymouth waited placidly for what might come, having long since relinquished all ambitions of his own. Wade grinned widely, expecting sport. "Read it, for Christ's sake, Philly," Rose said.

Philly laid the pages down, never taking his eyes off them, and straightened the lapels of his jacket. "What's the name of it?" he said.

"Doesn't have a name," the tourist said, still under the table.

Albert figured it was the safest place for him.

Philly straightened his whole girth, held the manuscript firmly in front of him and read exactingly, euphoniously, with kind conviction, pausing at the periods, submitting to the rhythms, a narrative of a man getting up in the morning, preparing himself for the day.

Everyone was entranced. Even the tourist sat up and gaped. By the second page Wade turned up his thumbs and grinned broadly. Albert in amazement settled back to enjoy. Weymouth woke up and Rose was transported. At the bottom of the third page Philly looked at the tourist for more.

"That's all," the tourist said.

"All?" Philly roared. "Well it's not bad. Far's it goes."

"I've been waiting all my life to write it," the tourist said.

"I've got a typewriter you can borrow. I used to write poetry. I'll show you some of my poems," Rose said.

"All right," the tourist said, admiring his fortunes. First the job, now this busty poet no less who had picked him up practically the moment he entered the place, not to mention the good drunk, the prospect of long good drinking and talk. He no longer felt broken and bruised. He had nothing to do for the next few days but decide. If he took the job he wouldn't have to start at once either. He could stay here a while.

"Albert, if you don't stop reading you'll never write anything," Wade said. "I wasted my life chasing cunt."

"You lying son of a bitch," Rose said.

"I like to drink beer myself," Weymouth said.

Philly said in a fury, "You sit at your little window, you watch the world go by. That's right, isn't it, Weymouth?"

"I have a penchant for small facts," Weymouth said, his face rosy as a baby's. "James Whitcomb Riley and Ella Wheeler Wilcox became engaged by correspondence but the marriage was never consummated."

Rose and the tourist, having pooled their quarters, went bumping arm-in-arm to the jukebox and a philosophical silence fell while all toyed with their various smokes and drinks.

"That reminds me of something I saw once," Philly said at last. "It was in Armenia. I was with this remittance woman. She had a van. We'd just met, you know, and right away she'd put me in charge, handed over the keys and credit cards. The day before I'd parked around the corner and when we came out of the restaurant the doors were gone.

So we were driving into the next village in this doorless van and we ran into a funeral procession. Somebody's child had died and the father was carrying it on his head in a coffin. It was just this little box, about three feet long. After him came a whole string of adults in single-file, mostly women, and then all these children acting happy. They were dressed in flowers, they were all decked out in their best clothes. They were laughing and playing, they were chasing each other in and out of peoples' legs and running around and around the father like they were entwining him."

"There's something," Albert said.

"I never got over it," Philly said, wistful for a moment.

59

FANG

When I was an undergraduate at Yale I was invited to dinner by a young lady who had a German shepherd of which she was inordinately proud and which she had trained herself out of a book. Naturally she wanted to put it through its paces. She made it lie down and get up and heel and all that good stuff.

Then she said Wrap a towel around your arm and take me by the throat. When I yell Fang he'll grab your arm. I demurred. It was a big dog you know, it had a splendid set of teeth. Oh it's all right she said I trained him myself. Well I was 26 and did not wish to appear anything but bold before this young lady so I wrapped a towel around my arm and then put my overcoat on over that and took her by the throat. She shouted Fang and the dog jumped up and bit her arm. You see she'd trained the beast herself.

FROSH

These two black guys
robbed me of my dope
in the dorm after I
invited them in.
They threw me against
the doorjamb and smashed
out my 4 front teeth. I
never thought I'd
get hurt, I didn't
think it could happen
to me, I'd never been
away from home, I wasn't
afraid of them
at all.

61

SEVENS

I had my horoscope cast on a cassette by an astrologer in New York. I sent him the information, he detests me, I detest him, we don't communicate. It was very appropriate to me in general, I was very impressed. My mother came to visit and I played it for her. It starts off: This is the chart of a subject born November 10th 1927 at 7 am. My mother gave a gasp. She said But you were born at 7 pm. That's an important difference you know.

Anyway I'm just entering a crucial phase of my life and I want all the help I can get, I want a clear head. I'm trying to figure out if I should have an affair with this Taurus. It's going to mean the end of my marriage if I do, or maybe it'll only be symbolic. My husband and I got a divorce last March but somehow I never really accepted it. We still sort of see each other on the sly, his girlfriend doesn't like it.

Now though everything's going to change. I also met this woman, she's a Libra, I like her quite a lot too. I wonder how it would be to have them both. Mother's quite hip about these things. She says whatever you do is all right so long as no one gets hurt.

The main thing about a menage is, will it work? Love isn't always enough. The Taurus has a Scorpio Moon, that's fantastic luck, and a Virgo rising. That'll produce a clash or two or maybe not. The Libra's Moon's in Pisces, with an ascendant Leo, so they're either opposite or the same and both attract or repel if Mercury gets involved. Mother's a Sagittarian with a mean Jupiter which she reserves for men, I have to admit. There's a lot of loose Aries in all this, it would be a very heavy atmosphere, it might be just fine.

I'm probably greedy. That's my Saturn in Cancer, but it makes sense too, like it's working for me. I want total synchronicity and why not since my next few years are supposed to be favorably aspected in every area and at every level. I'd be a fool to go on tiptoe. This reincarnation only lasts once. Well things will harmonize or they won't. It depends if I'm ruled by my higher or lower stars. Sometimes I can't tell which is which. I need a guru I guess.

63

ACCIDENT

I got run over on my bicycle the other day. It was Sam Martin, he's a Selectman you know. He got out, I was lying on the ground, he was all apologetic, he was very worried you know, it was obvious it was his fault, he was drunk. So I said you know I'm all right, go on home. He said Well you'd better report it to the police. There were some people standing around. He said If you're not all right let me know, I've got insurance, and then he drove off. So I went over to the police and told them what happened. When they found out who it was they didn't even write it down. They said you know If you have any trouble go see him, he'll take care of it, you don't need us.

Next day I had a stiff neck, I couldn't even turn my head, I thought there was something really wrong with me, so I went over to his house. I said you know I just wanted to let you know. He said Are you trying to give me a hard time? I didn't hit you, you hit me, I've got witnesses. Don't try to pressure me, get out of my house. He was really ugly, his wife was standing behind him in the hallway. I was scared so I left. I was going to tell the police, then I remembered all the things that happen to people on TV who get involved, and I said to myself I can't be bothered.

64

THE LIFE

That's the hardest work I ever done in my life. I was a steel pourer in Pittsburgh, that was nothin to this. You're down in the hold fillin baskets with fish, thirty tons a fish, you're up to your knees, I didn't even have no boots. You stickum in the basket with this gaff, then you handum up through the hatch. Somc guy's up there eatin donuts. I filled one of um too full, big fuckin fish fell out and hit me on the head. Hey! First time in my life I ever got hit on the head with a fish. Those baskets must weigh fifty pounds, I thought I was gonna die down there. I was so stiff I couldn't get outa bed this mornin, but I'm gonna try it again oner these days, it can't get any harder, it's gotta get easier, I musta learned somethin huh? Some fuckers don't like to work, I do. You work your day, you get paid, noner this weekly shit, you go get drunk a coupla days, you get broke, you go back to work again, that's the life.

?

I dreamt I was the king's daughter and lived in a tower and a herald came and said Your father's dead. I said All right.

Then the herald came back—there was no impression from his visit that he would —with two bodies under a sheet. He cut them up in pieces, stew size, and laid them out in plastic sacks under my mattress and I had to sleep on them for weeks and they began to stink. Now what do you think of a dream like that?

66

FLUFFY

I'm never going to have another pet, I had a little white dog once, I had him 15 years, he always slept on my bed. Finally his hind legs gave out and he made a mess wherever he went, he just dragged himself around, I had to clean up the house all the time, the bed was awful.

So I called the Animal Rescue League, that was after I lost my husband, and Mr. Costa came over and looked at him. He said His eyes and ears are good for his age, he's just old, I can't do nothing for him, you should let me put him out of his misery. That was the last thing I wanted to hear, I cried, the tears were running down my face, I said I can't see that. He said Well if you want me let me know.

He used to come in the restaurant, every time I saw him it would make me cry. You know what it's like being a waitress, I'd get home exhausted and give Fluffy a bath, and then I'd have to take a bath myself.

So finally I put him in a big galvanized tub in the yard with some old clothes in it. I gave him a bath every day until I couldn't stand it any longer, I was too tired.

My daughter-in-law didn't want me to put him to sleep but I called Mr. Costa, I had to. He said I'll pick him up tomorrow. She couldn't stand it, she took the kids away. I didn't want to be there either, I was going to be at work.

When I came back he was still there, Mr. Costa didn't come until after supper. The tears were running down my face, he said This is the best thing, you've only prolonged his misery. I didn't want to hear that, I thought maybe I've been wrong. He said I'll do it for you, I won't hurt him. Everything he said made me cry.

Next day he came in the restaurant, he was only trying to be nice, he said You don't have to worry, I cremated him, I spread his ashes in a nice place. That was the last thing I wanted to know, I got crying all over again.

I swore I'd never have another pet, I'm an old woman, I couldn't stand to go through that again, they're too much trouble. Once I almost got a poodle, he was so cute, but I didn't, maybe I should've.

68

THANKSGIVING

We went to my parents' house for Thanksgiving. We forgot what day it was, we never know what day it is, it's 1,200 miles, it worked out fine, we left Wednesday night and got there just as they were sitting down to dinner. They treated us tremendously, freaked me out, they gave us a room of our own, they were nice the whole time.

Winter

TOO

You're still here!
You're still here, too!

70

ON THE TABLE

Three bowls and spoons, three cups, a plate with a pit on it, two volumes of a ten volume set of Edgar Allan Poe, a Simenon, a wrench and pliers, a can of tobacco, a can of pot, an oil lamp, a knife, three pipes and a pot of chives.

THE FAMILY WAY

When I got to Scranton I called the number and some woman said What're you wearing, I'll be wearing a red wig and a yellow hat. I went out to wait and just down the block I remember a movie was playing called *The Family Way*. She was driving a copper colored Falcon and she had a sequined poodle sewn on her sweater, she was a beautician, her name was Agnes. We couldn't go back because her brother was painting the porch so we went to a shopping center and looked at furniture and then we went to the A&P. I was scared, I didn't know what was going to happen to me and I almost got sick when the butcher began quartering her chickens.

Then she locked her keys in the trunk with the groceries so we had to find a garage to get it open. Her brother was still painting the porch so she snuck me in the back door and put me upstairs in the bedroom. Her sister Marjorie was down in the living room with her son, he was about my age, watching basketball on TV. She was a nurse, she was huge, she was like a pyramid and she had her hair up in tight little pin curls, I never saw her smile the whole time.

They let me come down when their brother left but they didn't talk to me. Marjorie sits there reading *Life* magazine, she wets her finger each time she turns a page, she takes exactly the same amount of time on each page, about two seconds, she goes through the whole magazine that way, and right in the middle, she doesn't even look up, she says to Agnes How far along did she say she was? Agnes says Four months. And Marjorie says Looks like more than that to me, and I thought Oh God.

That night they had to pick up someone else at the Holiday Inn. We drove around and around but we couldn't find the right door and they didn't dare ask at the office. They left me in the car for about an hour while they hunted for her, her name was Hope, she was a telephone operator, she was dumb. She didn't have anything with her and neither did I, no one told me how long it would take, I was 18, so they took us to a store so we could get a toothbrush and a nightgown. When we looked around we couldn't find Agnes and Marjorie, they were in the lamp department.

Next day another woman drove us to a house in the country. I guess she was gay, she had a golfing hat on and she talked out of the side of her mouth like this Hi I'm Dutchy. On the way we had to stop at Woolworths and look at aluminum Christmas trees.

The house belonged to this thin old Italian woman. She didn't speak English but her daughter did. There were some other women there watching Perry Como on color TV. Hope went first and came right back and I was relieved because I thought Well there's nothing to it.

I lay on the bed, I had to put my knees up and the Italian woman put the catheter in, it was about two feet long, but I didn't feel anything.

Then we spent the evening watching TV. People die that way but I didn't know it, nobody mentioned that, it's the most dangerous method. There was an older woman, she kept making coarse jokes, I didn't like her, she offended me, but next day she turned out to be very nice. I said to Hope What're you going to do if it doesn't take? I think that's the word I used, take. She was very calm, she said Oh it doesn't matter, I'm not going to worry about it, we'll just get married, we're going to anyway some day, but I wondered what sort of a baby it would be with that tube up there.

That night I couldn't sleep the pain was so bad. The woman who made all the jokes walked around with me and timed my pains, she'd had three children. In the morning I started having contractions and Dutchy took me into the bathroom and made me sit on the toilet. I've never been in such pain in my life, I began to wish I'd just die and get it over with. She kept saying Push, Push, Push. Once I had a kind of spasm and the catheter came out about four inches and she stuck it back in again. I kept looking at the squares on the linoleum floor, all I wanted to do was lie down on it, it looked cool. I was soaked with sweat and I kept slipping off the seat and all of a sudden, she didn't tell me what she was going to do, she pulled the catheter out and threw it in the waste basket.

Then a car came in the driveway, she ran to the window, then she raced downstairs, I guess she thought it was the cops, but it turned out to be Marjorie.

While she was gone I felt this bug rush of liquid and afterwards I lay down on the bed, I was exhausted. When Dutchy came back she said Do you want to look at it? I said No. Then she said Would you like to know what sex it was? I said No.

I didn't have anywhere to go so I called the couple in Providence who'd given me the number and said Do you think I could stay with you for a day or two? and they said they'd meet me.

The Italian woman's daughter gave me some green pills and said to take them if I started bleeding too badly but she didn't say how badly too badly was. I didn't see Hope again, something went wrong with hers.

Marjorie drove me to the airport but when I got out of the car I couldn't move, I just stood there, I was paralyzed, maybe it was all that pushing, I don't know, but I couldn't move my legs. She drove off but she must've seen me standing there because she came back. She was furious, she said What're you doing? I said I can't move. She said Oh no you don't, you can't do that, you're getting on that plane, and she began to drag me into the terminal.

After we took off the stewardess came around and gave me a cup of soup, it was the first thing I'd had to eat all day. We hit some air pockets and it kept slopping in my lap and the lady next to me was getting more and more annoyed and finally she said Why don't you *drink* it? I said Because it's too *hot*.

When the plane landed the blood had soaked through my thick napkin. By this time I was really frightened, and the couple drove me to their gynecologist. He had an office in a very respectable building, I was a mess, I was wearing the same clothes, I smelled, and his receptionist, she was very snooty, she said What's the matter with you, are you pregnant? That made me laugh. She had her hair all lacquered like a helmet and she had a red suit on and a lot of bracelets. I said I'd rather not tell anyone but the doctor if you don't mind. She said You have to tell me, it has to go on the records anyway, and she sort of implied that she could find out any time she wanted to, and I said Well I'd *still* rather not.

She was quite nasty about it but she let me in. The doctor was disgusted. He said You've got yourself in quite a jam haven't you my girl? He examined me and said You'll have to go to the hospital, I'll have to notify your parents. I said Oh no, that's why I've been through all this. He wouldn't do anything for me, he wouldn't even advise me unless I gave him their name and number.

Well I wasn't going to do that so I tried another gynecologist in the same building. He was young, he was very nice, he asked me a lot of questions, what they'd done and if the conditions seemed sanitary and so on, and he looked up the pills in a book and told me to take one every hour, they'd contract the uterus. When I told him about the first doctor he just shook his head.

On the way out I said to the receptionist How much do I owe you? She said Nothing. That was really nice, I'd already had to borrow $800, plus travel expenses. I went back to the apartment and next day I was all right. I'd rather not have to do *that* again.

OWL AT NOON

Walter and I went out for a walk. He was going for his first cobalt treatment in the morning and my lover had just come back from California which didn't make him feel any better and I had to cajole him into coming when I'd rather have gone alone.

It was a freak day, a hot stark December noon. It was as if we were the only people on the planet. We went by boarded-up houses, the wind was whining in the telephone wires, it was wonderful it was so desolate. Over these black hills, way in the distance, we could see the bay like a sliver of glass in velvet, harsh and unexpected. That was when he said I wonder what will be going on tomorrow at this time, and I had a sense of something familiar, something that would happen again and again, the way it was when I was born, the way it'll be when I die, something exact and still, I can't explain it.

Then we walked on the beach for a while, we didn't talk, things were tense between us. He kept his head down watching the highwater mark where the debris is, where the gulls scavenge. I wanted to face the wind and look at all that blue. On our way back, as we were entering the woods, he pointed out a rabbit hanging in a tree, and I want to tell you, man, if you can possibly avoid it don't die by owl.

THEFT

My hat got stolen last night at Piggy's. I had a rainbow hat, it was a spectacular hat if I do say so myself, I had it sticking out of my hip pocket. I was standing at the bar, the place was packed, everybody was dancing you know and all of a sudden this hand reached through the crowd and ripped it out of my pocket. I chased him through the crowd, he ran out the door and jumped in a waiting van and drove off, they had it all planned. I don't even know what he looked like, I had my eye on the hat, I could see it you know in the dark.

MIDNIGHT

You know why I'm hanging around here at this time of night in the middle of the week? You know my 15 year old babysitter and her boyfriend? I just got back from my Women's Meeting and they were fucking on the couch. I said Well I guess I'll have to go out again for a little while. He says over his shoulder Bring us back a couple of meatball sandwiches when you come willya? So here I am. D'you think an hour's long enough?

SEE

Pals? Me and Suzie Speed, are you kidding? She's no pal of mine, I'm going to do her in, I'm going to make her a nice drink some day, next time she comes over. She sold me some pills, little yellow pills, for money too. I said What are they? She said You'll see. I said They ups, downs, what? She said You'll see.

So Hoodoo and I took one, all of a sudden it was like your head hit the moon, my body felt like a cloud of dust, all my nerves were dead, I couldn't move, these little motes were streaming through my brain.

I got scared, so did Hoodoo, I thought if this guy's scared I should really be scared, he takes everything, he's never straight. I says What's in the stuff, strychnine? He says I don't know man, nothing like this ever happened before.

Actually it was quite a trip, I wouldn't want to do it again though. I would've gone to the Drop-in Center but I couldn't face that, this 35 year old you know freaking out on drugs. There'd be some 14 year old chick on duty, she'd say Uh-huh, uh-huh.

Hoodoo put the pills in an envelope on the top shelf of the medicine cabinet for stuff you shouldn't take under any circumstances. Some day Suzie Speed's going to come by for a drink. I'm going to grind up the rest of those pills, there's about 10 left, and put them in it. She'll say What's this? I'll say You'll see.

78

YOUTH

My father and I were butting heads and art school was getting boring and I wanted to get away. He wanted me to get married and respectable, all my life I had to struggle against that. I had a friend in the same situation, a kid from a tough German family, we happened to be going by a recruiting office and he said Let's join the army. I said You must be mad. He said Why not? It was so spontaneous, we just did it.

I really had no talent or inclination for it but after Basic Training they put me in Special Forces. I was this frail little thing, I was scared to death. Special Forces I said That's Entertainment isn't it? That's Special Services the Sergeant said. You're Special Forces. Special Forces I said What's that? He said That's Airborne Guerilla Warfare and Commandos. What? I said They must be mad, there must be some mistake. They're so stupid.

It's all secret, clandestine, sabotage, murder, whatever. They're big on languages too. When you go to an area people think you're their friend just by virtue of speaking their tongue. The hard-cores put a lot of pressure on me to go airborne, I was the only one that didn't, there was a lot of harrassment. When're you going to go airborne, when're you going to go airborne? For two years I refused. I said I'm not jumping out of any airplanes, I didn't volunteer for this outfit.

We went on an Exfiltration Exercise. Twelve men paddling a raft out from the beach, we're supposed to rendezvous with a submarine, it's night, we're all dressed in black, it was like a spy movie. You can't dangle your feet, the sharks might get them, I love the water. When you locate the periscope you lasso it and they tow you out and take you in. It's spooky, this huge black thing coming up out of the black water. My whole four years in the army was like a fantasy, a dream. I said to myself What am I doing on a submarine, I don't belong here. We were down four days. All we did was eat, their food is delicious. Filet mignon for breakfast, cooked to order. They treated us royally. Then we all sat in the raft on the bow and the sub went down. All of a sudden there was nothing there. You feel so isolated. Well it's quiet and peaceful I'll say that much.

Then we got shipped to Okinawa. I got in with the Colonel, I drank with him, I drove his car. I was the brainy type, I could type, I always fraternized with the officers because I knew they could do things for you, I don't really mean that. One day I was down on the flight line and I saw this plane that said Origin: Okinawa, Destination: Iran. I said to someone Does this plane really go to Iran? He said Yeah once a week.

It blew my mind, I couldn't believe my luck, I was determined to go because I wanted to see my uncle in Teheran who was like a father to me. It took me six months. I fought and I schemed and I connived, I spent every minute planning it. I had to send my passport all over the world to get visas, there were a million forms to fill out, I saved up 45 days of leave.

When I put my papers in they came back stamped Disapproved. I demanded to know why. The Lieutenant was this hideously moronic idiot from Missouri. He said That's too long. I cited a regulation. Then he said Nobody's ever gone that far, it's too far to travel. He was afraid I'd never come back. He said Why don't you go to Tokyo like everyone else? I said I've got 45 days coming to me and I'm going to Iran. He said No you're not. I said Yes I am. He said Oh no you're not. I said I am whether you like it or not Sir. He said Don't forget I have to approve it.

So I called the Colonel, he came down and fixed me up, no hassles. At the last minute the Lieutenant said Besides you have to have enough money to come back by commercial airline in case there's no Space Available. I took out the $600 I'd saved and laid it on his desk so finally he had to sign my papers.

I was all set to go when the Laotian Crisis came up. The Philippines were full and all vacation travel was cancelled. I said Oh no. I went to see this Major I'd taken French with. He said Don't use my name but there's a secret flight going tomorrow morning at eight. Just say you have access to classified information. So I went down there next morning with my bag. The Sergeant said How'd you know about this flight, you're not supposed to know about this flight. He wouldn't let me on. So I found the pilot and I said Listen I've been planning this for six months, I won't tell a soul, I swear to god. He looked at me and I said Please. He said Grab your bag and get on the plane and don't say a word to anyone.

When we got to Clark AFB I called a Captain I used to know. He said Come and stay at my BOQ, don't worry. He introduced me to everyone as his cousin and got me on the first plane to Bangkok.

The Flight Clerk there turned out to be an Arab. He said Your papers are all here, you're really well-prepared, this is amazing, most people are missing something. I said I've been planning this for six months, I explained everything to him. He said There's no Space Available but since you're so well-prepared I'll book you all the way to Iran as an Official Passenger so you can't get bumped.

Everybody got off at Karachi. I waited around the cafeteria with the pilot drinking coffee, we were talking Arabic. After a while he looked at his watch and we went out to the plane. There was no one there. I said Where's everyone else? There isn't anyone else he said The flight is yours, and he bowed.

Bankok, Saigon, Calcutta, New Delhi, Karachi, Teheran. I can't believe the determination I had, you want things so bad. Youth is incredible that way.

81

EMBASSY FLIGHT

That's the way they do things. We left Hawaii in our wool winter uniforms and when we landed on Okinawa it was 110.

It was this dilapidated old junkheap, I couldn't hear for a week after, halfway over one of the engines gave out. We had to wait fourteen hours while these two guys worked on it. Finally the Sergeant says You can take your coats off. He wouldn't let us take off our ties.

So they filled it up with fuel and loaded us all on. There were ninety passengers on a plane with a capacity of sixty, all with their eighty-eight pounds of luggage not the forty-four allowed, nuns, natives, chickens, soldiers, everybody.

They didn't even test the engine, they just took off. About two minutes later this same engine went kopple-gobble-clock, and died.

We're flying around and around over the ocean on three engines trying to get it going again. So then they said Well we'll have to dump 18,000 gallons of fuel so we can land, I could just see them pouring it out the portholes in buckets. Then I looked out the other window, there was this black stuff coming out of one of the engines, just clouds of it. I said to myself Oh no. I called the stewardess and pointed out the window. I said I think it might be you know oil. She turned stone white and said Oh it's probably nothing serious, I don't think it's anything to worry about. I learned later it was her first flight, she was trying to keep me calm. Then she ran, she galloped to the cockpit and came back with the Flight Engineer. He took one look and said Thank you to me, he was very formal, he bowed and went back to the cockpit, he didn't run, he walked, he wasn't taking his time though.

By now everybody's onto the situation, the nun beside me's got her beads out, she's doing the whole bit, the Sergeant takes a pint out of his hip pocket and starts drinking to his death. Then they said Get in crash position, head down, no smoking.

I thought Well here you go, it had to happen sooner or later, you may as well accept it. We landed all right, bump and grind, nobody even got hurt. One guy when he got out got down on his knees and began kissing the runway, he was so relieved.

83

VIENTIANE

Elephants and temples and fantastic trees. We were trying to get the Montagnards, woo them. We drank rice wine out of coconut shells through long straws and really got stoned. They're beautiful people, they have red hair. We got chased out by the Pathet Lao. They shot at our encampment one night. Boy did we make tracks.

•

He's been picking me up
in the A.M. and we smoke
some of that dope
so the rest of my day
is all fuckin disoriented.

•

The only one in six
experts that made
any sense said Sex
isn't everything in life,
only a part, only a small
part of it. I wish I
believed that.

SEASON'S GREETINGS

Every year I get a card from these friends of mine from college, I haven't seen them in about seven years. It always has a Christmas tree on it and inside there's this string of names. Marvin and Donna, Sally, Bill, Tom, you know. They're very conventional people, Mr. & Mrs. Straight.

I got this sudden urge to communicate with them. I started a letter, I said you know How're you, I'm fine and tried to tell them what I've been doing. It was all lies. I wrote half a page and tore it out of the typewriter.

I didn't know what to do, send them a picture of my prick or what. I wanted to say Where are you? Wake up! I can't imagine what they'd think of this commie hippie long-haired Jew faggot they used to know.

So finally I just wrote Justice in my life, perfection in my art, this is what I strive for. Pablo Casals. Then I wrote Me too. Pray for peace in 1973.

85

DREAM WITHOUT CLIMAX

I was at a bus stop near a park, I would just walk by on my way somewhere else, school I guess . There was a box on the bench with a sliding cover like a matchbox, only it had a flap inside. I opened it but I had it upside down and whatever was in there almost fell out, so I turned it over and opened the flap. There was a baby inside, it had this gnarled red face, it was like a little mummy thing. I fed it or rubbed it or did something friendly and then closed the box again. I kept coming back every day and opening the box and one day there was a second baby. I could see they were related, they looked alike, they were brothers maybe. Once the youngest jumped out of the box and ran across the street and I couldn't catch it and had to coax it back. I was always opening the box upside down and one time this voice said Please don't do that, you're hurting our faces. Oh I said I'm sorry, I'll try not to do it again. That's all there was, there was no climax.

CHARACTER IN ASPEN

It's horrible there now, I used to love it. All the old miners are gone, everything's changed. It's turned into a ski resort, soak the tourists. All my friends out there are into making money and the cowboys drive pickup trucks with gun racks in them, they go around looking for longhairs to beat up. There used to be one old guy who always took his horse into the saloon with him and when it shat he held his hat under it, he was a real character.

FAUX PAS

I'd never seen one before,
I was 17 and naturally
all I did was wonder
about it. It seemed
it must be huge, I just couldn't
imagine. I was on this date,
the guy took his out, I
don't know why, I kept looking
at it, I almost said That's not
such a big thing. Lucky for me
I didn't.

NORTH CAMBRIDGE

I hadn't been home in about three months so one day I got it together and called my mother. I said Get the turkey ready and the cake and ice cream. I was just joking you know. She said What time will you be home? Oh I said about noon. I was gonna hitch-hike, I left early enough. You know what she did? She got up at seven o'clock and cooked a turkey and baked a cake and bought some ice cream. You know what time I got there? One-thirty in the morning, and I was stinking drunk. I ate a little bit of turkey and some ice cream, I couldn't eat any cake, and then I passed out. My father wouldn't even talk to me, I couldn't talk anyway. My mother gave me a lot of shit about that next morning.

What happened was my ride went right by a bar I used to hang out in so I went in for a beer and all my old buddies were there. They were telling me about the kids in the neighborhood, seventeen-eighteen year olds, they all run in gangs now. They're very hostile, they think it proves their masculinity. They just hang around on the corner all day hoping somebody'll come by with a joint, they've got nothing else to do.

The cop on the beat's a real ballbuster. They throw bottles in the street, and then they wonder why he's such a bitch. He's just doin his duty, that's his job. So they rolled his son one night, they got three, four dollars. One of them had a blade, he's trying to make it into the gang so he slashes the kid a few times in the back, gave him 100 stitches in the hospital. So the kid mentions a few names, what's he supposed to do, keep his mouth shut when he gets carved up? Now they say they're going to kill him. Like it's all his fault, like he asked to have a cop for a father.

I get along with my parents all right. My father can't stand long hair though. If I was in the service he'd accept me. He manages an auto-body shop. He can't see anyone working less than 50 hours a week. All his friends do it, then they go home and watch TV and wash the car on weekends. I went to a community college for a year. It was just like high school, there was no social atmosphere like a university or anything. After class you'd sit in a drugstore and sip a coke and then go home, so I quit.

I happen to have an uncle in the phone company. He's an executive, he's been there 30 years. My father told him I wanted a job there, he didn't even ask me. It's good pay, you start at $150 a week and nobody works too hard, they start you on your pension plan the first day, you're supposed to be there the rest of your life, but you have to have references. It's like being spoken for by a politician. My uncle would've had to do it, I didn't want him to have to lie, so I split. That's how I got down here. My father still can't understand why I don't want to spend the next 40 years in North Cambridge.

HOLIDAY

I'm going on a three day jag, man.
My father's out right now
buying me a case of beer.
I'm not kidding.
He knows where I'm at.
He'll get me a couple a bottles
a vodka too and some anisette,
about a half a gallon. I
love that stuff. And a bottle
a Scotch for my mother, I'll
drink some a that. And a couple
a bottles a whiskey for my brother,
I'll drink some a that too. Oh
it's going to be a pisser.

90

NEW YEAR'S EVE

I had to work New Year's Eve, I'm just as glad, I was happy to, I mean it, I'm serious. I've had some real disasters on New Year's Eve and I thought What the hell I'll have a few quiet drinks and go home intact for once. Sam had to work too, he was glad too. Ciro's was deserted, we sat around all night swapping New Year's Eve horror stories, and at two-thirty we closed up and congratulated ourselves on our good luck and started home, I figured it was too late for anything to happen.

I saw him next day, he was in terrible shape. He was walking by a party and he went in and got drunk and fell down and smashed his face, his nose was all messed up, he just fell down and didn't get home until noon next day and the girl he was living with was furious and left him. So you never know, you can never tell, I guess you can never be sure you're safe until you're sitting down New Year's Day to the Rosebowl.

HASSLER

John Dice was giving Jane a hard time
at the bar. She was very polite, very
nice, just as she always is. She's
ready to sympathize with anyone.
You know John Dice, it only egged him on,
he got worse and worse, he kept asking
about her cunt. All of a sudden she
turns to me, she says Is this guy a pro?
Oh yes I said. She says Don't you dare
attack me you filthy little man
and he left her alone after that.

92

BACK

First thing I did was put away my watch. I've just been sitting around watching it snow, reading a little, writing a little, getting back into it. I haven't been able to do much the last six months, I incurred some debts, circumstances of life, and I had to go back home and get a job, cooking in a restaurant, I really got into it, so it was okay, but I'm glad to be back, I'm sick of cities.

Flying's a real trip these days. All the airports are packed, long lines of people at every gate, armed guards everywhere. You have to go through this white tunnel, at the end there's a little ramp with a metal detector and a bunch of guards to search your hand luggage. One of the guards says to me, along with half a dozen others, Come this way please. I said All right.

He took us down this green tunnel. There were these stalls with Southern Fried Chicken buckets and another guard with a hand detector with a dial and a big loop. He holds it up to me like a Buck Rogers ray gun and says You gota lota metal onya. He made us empty our pockets, all these freaked-out businessmen in suits dumping out their gewgaws and change. All I had left was my glasses, the brass studs in my belt, the zipper in my fly and my fillings. I had to go through the white tunnel again. The guy was very suspicious, he says You Pass but you still gota lota metal onya. And then if they don't find a bomb in your bag you can get on.

So I'm sitting on the plane, everyone's asleep, I figured what the hell I'll smoke a joint. So I went back to the bathroom and locked the door. I had two puffs and right away I got paranoid, I put it out. No one noticed, no one said a word. Later on I thought you know nothing's going to happen, no one's going to care. So I sat on the john and smoked the rest of it, I was really stoned. When I came out wouldn't you know there were all these businessmen waiting in line with nasty looks on their faces. The whole place reeked like a Turkish bath. Boy was I glad to get off that plane.

Coming back I got talking to the guy at the ticket desk, I showed him my rainbow flag, all those freaky colors. He wrote the flight number on the envelope and stapled a piece of paper on it. He said Sit up back and just show it to the stewardess. There was no ticket inside, he didn't charge me. She just nodded when she saw it. So there's still hope.

94

CHRIST

I was in a bookshop up on Orleans and I said to the owner Do you have Kate Millet's *Sexual Politics*? The woman said This is a Christian bookshop. Well I said I'm very interested in Women's Liberation. Do you have anything at all in that line? And the woman said Christ is our liberator.

95

ANONYMOUS

I was hitching back to college, this black and white car stops, I was always afraid of something like this but I wasn't thinking about it, I had an exam coming. We had the usual conversation about the weather, he's a workingman in his middle thirties, old-looking with these black glasses and light eyes, all of a sudden he reached in his pocket and pulled out a knife. He grabbed me around the head with the knife at my throat, I got the door open, one foot's hanging out, the car's swirling, he says Put your head in my lap and you won't get hurt. I panicked, I did what he told me, the tip of his knife kept pushing in my throat. I said What do you want?

He kept saying Do what I say and you won't get hurt. I kept talking trying to find out what he intended to do, my voice was shaking. He said I want to ball you. I said I'll do anything you say if you'll promise to let me go. There's more talk, more bargaining, he stops the car, I'm going crazy trying to think what to do.

There's a path into the woods. I can see him deciding not to leave the knife in the car, I figure he's going to kill me. He said Don't scream, and put a blue stocking cap over my face and pulled me out the driver's side. He said Are you engaged, how old are you, do you have a boyfriend? I lied, I played innocent, I said I've never had sex, I'm only 20.

I tried to run but he grabbed me and held the blade of the knife hard across my throat. He said Why did you try to run, don't look at my face. He laid our coats on the ground, he says We must do it the right way. He undressed me and took off his pants, he stuck his fat hands up my vagina. He says We're going to do 69. I played stupid, I said What's that? I made him show me. He got angry, he said Pretend I'm your boyfriend, put more into it. I kept watching the knife, I thought if he tries to cut me I'll fight for my life, I'll fight hard. I should've bit it off, the whole of it, next time I will. I thought I'm going to die, there's nobody to help, no one knows.

My mind lapsed in and out of consciousness, I was so sad to lose my life. It flickers in my memory, riding in the car head down, walking into the woods, my feet were heavy, the snow was deep. He said When I come swallow it. Then he said Put your clothes on, and I thought he's going to let me go. He said I didn't want to get you pregnant, he left me there.

I was hysterical, screaming, crying, gagging, I began to run for help down this dirt road. A car came, I hid, it was him, he gave me back my books. He said Don't tell the police. There was no license on the car, I lost my glasses.

Everybody's door was locked. Finally a woman came, at first she wouldn't let me in to use her phone. No answer, no answer. Her daughter gave me a ride to my sister's house, she hugged and kissed and kept me warm, I was safe. The police came and asked questions, they never caught him. My parents never found out.

After that I couldn't sleep, all I could do was go to the movies, I couldn't watch them, I'd get up and go to another, I was frightened, I cried a lot, I ate all the time, my nerves were terrible. Then the anger came, and then the hate.

HARDER THAN HEGEL

You probably think I'm unhappy.
Of course I'm unhappy.
I'm miserable, why shouldn't I be?

Are you happy? Maybe there's something
wrong with you. I'm a rotten bastard,
everybody knows it, why should I pretend?

The sun comes up, the sun goes down,
the world is flat or round.
A man's only duty is to die gracefully.

Till then what does it matter?
I'm happy sometimes but I prefer misery.
Why shouldn't I? At least I understand it.

98

THE PITS

He did not seem to be involved in the conversation, he seemed to be simply ignoring everything, and sat, chin in hand, elbow on his knee, for several minutes before he finally got off his stool and came down to the other end of the bar where Sara was waiting. He was grey as a stone.

"Walter, will you cash a check?" she said.

"No," he said as if he meant it.

"You mean you'd make me go to the Fo'c's'le at this hour of the evening?"

"Why not? I'd like to go there myself."

"Walter, you look tired tonight," she said, writing the check.

"What'll you have?" he said dryly.

"Scotch, please," she said and laughed with pleasure.

"That'll be $5.90," he said.

"I went to that new breakfast place you told me about," she said.

"Without me? Rotten Sara!"

"Walter, how much Scotch are you giving me?"

"Mind your own business. It's just because I love you. I'd love to beat you."

"You could add a little water. Has it been busy?"

"Busy? Oh yes. The last two days. It's the pit of the year, everybody's drunk and hostile."

"It's been such nice weather."

"Outdoors, yes," he said.

She sat down at a table and took her coat off, an orange thing with the stuffing coming out.

Walter poured a shot-glass full of Scotch, came through the door back of the bar and sat down beside her.

"Oh, are you going to sit with me?" she cried delightedly.

"I'll take a little respite," he said, drinking half the Scotch, but he got up instantly, wearily, cleared the empty glasses and bottles from the next table, set them on the bar and sat down again. "Liz and Sally have been talking about automobiles all night, I didn't think I could stand it another minute."

"They want to buy one?" Sara said. "They have one to sell?"

"How much horsepower, what model, the year," Walter said. "The things people talk about! You can't imagine the things I have to listen to. They don't even know I'm there."

"It's been such nice weather," she said, "we ought to organize a picnic on the point."

"I hate that word. I had a wife who organized everything."

"In what way?"

"I'd say, 'I've got to shit'. She'd say, 'It's not 7:10 yet.'"

"I never knew you were married."

"Sure. Everybody does it once. Well, not everybody."

"How about Wednesday, that's my day off," Sara said. "I'll make a lunch."

"That'll be marvelous," Walter said, nodding. "I haven't been out there in two years—the last time you took me, in fact. Let's hope it's warm and sunny!"

"It doesn't matter," she said, "the jeep's got both doors on again."

"All the same," he said.

"Walter, it'll be a beautiful day," she said. "It's been awfully busy?"

"Busy?" he said, touching his chin. "Last night I thought I saw an unfamiliar face and I asked Jingles, but he said no."

"You have to wait for April for that," she said.

"I don't know if I'll make it," he said.

"You'll make it," she said.

A new waiter with a neat little beard came up from the restaurant downstairs and impatiently began looking around for the bartender.

"What can I do for you?" Walter said.

"Can I have a glass of water?" the waiter said.

"You can get it yourself," Walter said. "I'm not getting up for that."

The waiter raised his eyebrows, then went up and down the bar looking for an entrance but there wasn't any, and he came back annoyed.

"You have to go through that door," Walter said.

"Most gross," the waiter said and went in.

"Most gross?" Sara said, making a face.

"I'll have to have a talk with that young man some day," Walter said.

Inside the bar the waiter filled a glass with ice and squirted it full of soda water, then threw it all in the sink.

"Where's the water?" he called.

"Where it always is," Walter said. "In the sink."

The waiter filled the glass from the faucet and looked up. "You're better at this than I am," he said.

"I can believe it," Walter said.

"I see you've got ouzo," the waiter said contritely. "I ought to have some of that. It makes me clear-headed and then I fall down."

"You're doing pretty well on water," Walter said, finishing his Scotch. "Well. Back inside the hotdog stand."

"I'm really glad you came out," Sara said. "I wanted to talk to you but not at the bar. You must have got my messages."

"Well, sometimes I come out and it really surprises people," he said. "I had to get away from there for a minute."

He opened the door and turned back. "People ought not to take me for granted," he said. "Ought not to take anyone for granted."

"You ought to treat everyone like a new lover," Sara said.

"Yeah," he said, grinning in the door. "Or a good old one."

He went inside the bar and washed the glasses and threw the bottles in the waste bin with a crash, then poured himself another Scotch. He glanced up to find her eyes on him and he took a sip and winked. "Vitamin B-12 is good stuff too," he said, went back to the other end of the bar where the people were and sat on his stool.

DREAMS OF AN ITALIAN HAIRDRESSER

They say if you dream on Thursday it'll come true, I don't know, the younger generation don't believe in those superstitions any more, still you start to wonder sometimes.

My aunt dreamed my brother was playing ball and the ball went over a fence around some high frequency wires and he climbed over after it and got electrocuted. My uncle kept saying Don't worry about it, don't worry about it. My brother was supposed to come for supper so when he didn't come she called the police but they didn't know anything. So after we ate my uncle said Well get in the car, it's true, he's over in Hoboken. He didn't want to spoil her supper.

Another aunt dreamed a black child came to her in a vision and said Who'd you rather have die, your mother or your father, if one of them had to and you had to choose? So she said I'd rather my father didn't die, we have a big family, we need someone to support the children. And her mother was dead in a month.

It's stupid but it happened in Provincetown because that's where I met him, it wasn't too recently ago. I was going out with this guy down here. One of my customers back in Hoboken had a dream, I don't know if it was a Thursday, she said that her boyfriend, he was a divorced man like mine, said to her We have nothing, my wife and I at least have our children. She came in a week later and said he'd married his wife again. The same thing happened to me. Could be a coincidence but it seemed weird. I wouldn't want to live here all the time, you never meet anyone in the winter.

102

MY LITTLE BROTHER

I went home for a month. My little brother, he's 20, he's really been catting around, coming in at dawn and sleeping all day. It was freaking my mother out so one night to teach him a lesson she locked the door to his bedroom, it's right across the hall from hers, she sleeps with her door open, there was no way he could get in without waking her up, and there're burglar bars on all the windows.

Next morning he was nowhere in the house and his door was still locked, my mother was really freaking out, she thought he hadn't come home at all, so about noon my father said Why don't you look in the bedroom, maybe he found some way to get in. So she opened the door and there was my brother sound asleep. This kept happening every night. My mother was totally freaked, she had to give up, she said I won't say anything if you'll tell me how you get in. My little brother said You know I'd get more sleep if you wouldn't lock me out. It takes me an hour to get the bars off the window and another hour to put them back on again.

SMOKE COOLS

My father died, that was the end of me. I was very close to him, his only girl. He loved my little brother too. I looked up to him. I always thought, What would he think?

He died of lung cancer, it all went through him. He smoked a lot. It got into his liver, it got into his nodes, it got into his bones. He suffered for weeks, night and day. No drug could help him. When it reached his brain he convulsed. I had to lie on top of him, he died with me holding him down.

I'll never be the same, the spine went out of all our lives. I never had another happy day, everything went wrong. There was never a day when I didn't miss my dad. I needed him.

My mother lost everything. She took up with well a gigolo. She was young, she'd been very sheltered. My father left us fixed, his whole life went into it, a bank account, insurance, a house, a car, a summer cottage, all in good condition, everything anyone could want.

They went through it all, they had these huge expensive parties. I wouldn't even go near the house finally. I had a nervous collapse, everybody has a breaking point. I don't even know where my mother is now, the gigolo's long gone.

I think, Why? When I see guys walking around on the street, much older guys, my father was 53, drunks, bums, useless scum, I ask why God lets these things happen. I asked the priest. You have to have faith it makes a larger sense, he said. I've never set foot in a church since.

My litle brother, 17, got his girlfriend pregnant and had to marry her. Dad never would have let that happen. They moved in with me and my husband and our three kids. They wouldn't go home either. They didn't have a cent and no job, we were supporting them.

I went by the cottage one night. I looked in the windows. Other people were living inside, like a dream. I thought, We should be there.

My husband couldn't stand it, he went to Florida. He got a job and a house, all furnished, and he called me up. I went down with the kids. I abandoned my little brother.

I couldn't equal my father. He worked all the time, he never stopped worrying, he kept us all from harm. He'd die if he knew. When I saw him going down in that hole in the ground I thought, Why? There has to be a reason.

I smoke, I've got asthma too, I can hardly breathe sometimes. I'll die just the way Dad did. I still do it, I don't care. He was his own man, he had a lot of dignity. I will too.

I lost the house in Florida when I came up to see how little brother was doing. My husband begged me not to go, he got down on his knees, but I had to.

He and his wife were separated. She had the baby at home, her parents hate him. He was sleeping in a shed, he was on some kind of drugs.

I found a place for him and got him back to health. My husband couldn't stand it. He quit his job in Florida and gave up the house and came back and got sick for a year. He's better now. He can do anything but he can't get a job, he's gone back to Florida.

I haven't seen little brother in a month. I heard he left town. His wife's with an aunt in Medford, the baby's at her parents, the whole family's scattered.

Rent's due, I'm running out of food, all there is in the house is soup. The kids keep asking, Why do we always have soup? I've always fed them good.

Something's got to break for me soon. Can I have one of yours? Then I've got to go.

THE MAGNIFICENT NEW MUNICIPAL FOYER

The air conditioner went bats, it was down to 20 below, there were icicles hanging off the ceiling and walls. I panicked and turned the heat all the way up and locked the place for the weekend. On Monday all the ice had melted, there was water everywhere, it was like a furnace. I opened all the windows and mopped up all the water in time for the First Session, nobody noticed a thing.

One day I was standing there, right here in fact, and I heard a crack, I looked all around, I couldn't figure out what it was, there was this roar of plaster and tiles, I jumped back and cracked three ribs. I swept up the mess and went to the doctor, he taped me up, he says Don't move around much.

Next day I'm standing there, there's a roar, same thing happens, I jump back, I crack the ribs again. Inside a week all the fucking tiles fell off, I thought they was going to burn me for it, but five M.I.T. experts came down and said it wasn't my fault, it was the construction company, they used the wrong glue.

I went over to my sister's, I opened a beer, I says to myself What was I sweating, I don't have no $120,000 anyway.

106

STUPID BABY

for Everybody

Hey you fall down here? How come you fall down here where it's flat when you just got down the whole hill without even holding my hand? Stupid baby.

Oh that's the reason. There's ice under the snow. It's all icy here. That's why you fell down, look here under the snow, it's all icy here, that's why you fell down, stupid baby.

Spring

BEGINNING

I've got a $180 barbill at Ciro's. It happened last winter. I had about three drinks there one night and nobody I was with had any money so I said Jimmy can I put it on the tab and he said Sure. That was the beginning of the end.

SPRING BEAUTY

On warm Saturday afternoons in late April everybody's out on the street. There's a festive air, groups mingle and merge, and the blood gets going again. The sun lights new shingles and paint, familiar faces reappear, crocuses unexpectedly pop up where they always do and the shops get ready to open. Where last year a deli was, jewelry will be sold or leather, fancy trash or fudge. The Scene is gone with its trinket bins and rubber chickens, its madly-blinking lights and hard-hawking proprietor, but the Café Blasé survives. Handfuls of daytrippers troop up and down, and the locals gossip on the meatrack. You can hear the ring of hammers and laughter, and the old come out with their canes.

One such day Eddie was sitting in the window of the Fo'c's'le with two floozies from B.U. when his wife Sugar went by with the babies in the carriage. Her jaw fell, she turned white, swallowed, then turned red, looked straight ahead and rushed on toward her mother's: he was supposed to be clamming.

She went only half a block, her heart still as a rock, then ran back, bumped the carriage up over the curb, put her face to the glass. The babies' heads bobbed up, their eyes black as raisins.

Eddie never noticed, engrossed in buying the girls a drink. Exquisite visitants from the rich world, one was Chinese, the daughter of a mathematician, in white silks, with lips like cresting waves, the other a copperhaired Jew in a fur coat and jeans. They were interested in Eddie as a native: that night they would eat at Ciro's, get high on good wine and go dancing, but not with him. All the same he had his appeal, the casual beauty of his weathered body and marked face, the charm of his open obeisance, which impelled them to play with him a little.

Sugar put her hands on her hips, eyes agoggle. She opened her mouth but no sound came out. The babies peeped over the side and disappeared. Then she whirled off the other way toward home, went ten yards, returned on the run, jolted the carriage back up on the sidewalk and rapped on the window. She thought he's spending the paycheck too, he never spends a cent on me.

The sight of her knocked Eddie into a disappointed coma: he refused to believe his bad luck. What was she doing here? Why couldn't she leave him alone? It was his day off on top of everything else.

Sugar beckoned to him urgently, the outrage in her face giving way to amazement, then hurt, as he turned back to the oblivious girls. He thought I'll go live with them—but the hope lasted only a moment.

"You get out here," Sugar yelled.

His eyes grew fixed and he scowled. He sensed her dimly beyond the window, in a separate life. He thought, What does she want?

The huge bouncer impassively sucked ice by the door. His head did not move but his eyes took everything in. This was a second job for him: he was saving up for his honeymoon, after which he swore he would work no more on weekends.

Sugar came in like a hornet, spat at the Chinese girl, cuffed her husband, then got a hammerlock and tried to drag him off his seat but, suddenly overcome by shame, she ran out and wheeled the carriage down the street toward her mother's, decided to go home after all, came back so soon he had no relief from her absence. He sat unmoving, as if invisible. Indignant and guilty, the girls each turned a shoulder toward him.

Sugar paced in front of the window, incredulous, then strode in again and hit Eddie a serious whack on the side of the head. He didn't move or look at her, kept his hands folded on the table, solid as granite. She glared at the two girls and hit him harder. "You get home," she yelled. The girls glanced at her with sympathy, then away. The babies slept in the sun, their gnarled little faces sealed like pink fists.

Sugar set out for her mother's again, changed her mind once more and came back instantly, but there was no going by the three blurred figures in the window, and this time she started in for mayhem, but the bouncer eased up and put his foot across the door. His broad belly rested on his knee.

"You're flagged," he said.

"That's my husband, I've got a right to talk to him," she said, but he shook his head and looked phlegmatically over her at the great linden shimmering with new little leaves.

She couldn't budge his bulk, then leaned across his thigh and shouted at Eddie, "You goddamned son of a bitch of a bastard."

His eyes popped at her as if she were a lunatic.

"If you don't stop bothering the customers," the bouncer said.

She tried to barge past him. Angerless as a shrug, he took her by the shoulders and tossed her into the street, then blocked the doorway, elbows touching the sills.

She sat on the curb while the crowd flowed around her, nursing her scraped knees with some Kleenex, then got up wincing and without looking in the window again turned the carriage toward her mother's house and did not come back. In another moment the girls had joined the sunny crowd on the street and vanished, and Eddie moved to the bar and drank till he passed out.

MOULDERING OUT THERE FOR MONTHS

My late concubine the bitch
decamped with a Canadian poet.
I threw all her things
out the window, all her clothes,
her books, her yellow douche bag
like a damn crocus in the pile,
her 35 million hats. She was
a vile cook and lazy as the day
is long besides being an abominable
sentimentalist and a junkie. I
plucked her out of the gutter,
to the gutter she returns. Good
riddance! To tell you the truth
I don't think she's ever coming back.

112

YOU KNOW ME

My delicious lovely doctor, I'm so in love with him I can't believe it, but he's having an affair with his nurse, they make dates in front of me. He's always trying to get me to move out of Provincetown, that's the kind of guy he is, he's so straight. He says there's nobody here but hippies, he keeps reminding me of the VD rate. When I told him I was going to go on Welfare to pay for my operation he said That's not necessary at all, you could get a job if you really wanted one, you can, you can. If you really try and can't find a good job I'll eat my hat, I will, I'll eat my hat. He gave me $5 to put an ad in *The Advocate,* he made me take the money. On the way home, you know me, I bought a book, I'm just no good.

PRIORITIES

I was down on the wharf, I saw this beautiful girl, I sidled over you know we got talking and she says You know a cheap place I could stay tonight? I said Yeah, you know, You can stay with me. For Free. She said No. I didn't show any disappointment, I just went on talking like I didn't care. We walked a while and then she got in her car and left.

I saw her driving around later. She said you know Get in. I said Huh, all right. We drove around and I gave her the old line you know Come on home and see my etchings. It's hard to keep a straight face when you've got a houseful of etchings. So we wound up at my studio. I was lucky, I haven't had that beautiful a girl in a long time, never, I never had a woman like that.

I had a dinner invitation the next day, I didn't want to break it you know I said I'd come. We were lying in bed and I had to tell her. I said I'll only be gone a couple of hours. Come and go as you please, make yourself at home. When I got back she was gone. I never saw her again. I guess I should've stayed right where I was.

114

KENTUCKY

Did you ever see a man fuck a horse? I did down in Kentucky. I used to drink with these guys I worked with at the stables. There was a drive-in liquor store. Anybody was old enough if you were in a car. They had beer and whiskey, good whiskey too. You rolled down the window and they opened a hole in the door and you told them what you wanted and they gave it to you. Anyway they were always talking about it, that's all they talked about. I said I don't believe it, you're full of shit. So one night we were coming back from town, we lived near the stables, there was a mare and her foal in one of the stalls. One of the guys got a big oats bucket, he was very short, he piled another bucket on that and he did it, he fucked the horse. He put her tail up on her rump, she kept snorting through her nose. I thought it was very amusing at the time, I was so hysterical I could hardly even keep my balance. Anyway it was the end of the night.

115

ON THE BUS

I was on the bus, all I wanted to do was come. I couldn't read, I couldn't look out the window, I couldn't do anything, I was completely preoccupied. I kept thinking about men and how they must do it all the time. I mean you're always reading about them masturbating in movie-houses and stuff. There was nobody in the next seat, there was somebody across the aisle but she wasn't paying any attention so I put my raincoat over me like a blanket and pretended to go to sleep. I'm sitting there with this raincoat in my lap and my hand in my crotch. It took about two minutes, then everything was fine, my head was clear, I could think.

BUSTOUT

I grew up in East Texas. There's nothin to do there, I mean nothin. In summer you go skinny-dippin at night, in winter you sit around the drugstore readin movie magazines and hopin you're not pregnant, that's the range. Sorry.

I went to the University for a year, then I went to Yale for a year, I thought it was a big deal, the center of eastern culture and all that bullshit, I know better now, the whole time I never met one man that had any originality or elegance.

I wanted to find out where the energy was, I wanted to be where it's happening, but the whole East Coast is dead, nothin's real here. In every age there's always someplace where things converge, where the action is, so I started hitchin around, I ended up strippin in a Denver bustout joint. Can you imagine my disappointment? You're up in the mountains in this exotic scene, you figure it must be a very esoteric place, and then it turns out the whole town's full of Fort Worth oilmen.

Charles the owner started out with whorehouses in East Texas, then he began buying bustout joints in Denver but sex isn't much of a commodity any more, it's too easy to come by, everybody's giving it away, he's very shrewd, he knows that, so now he's buying supperclubs in California. He might be a brother of John Connolly, he's got those silver-grey temples and just buckets of Texas charm. Connolly's got a little more polish maybe, there's not much to choose between them, it's exactly, this is important, it's exactly the same distance to Washington DC and Denver. Life's like that.

I've got half a novel done but it's probably too raunchy to publish, I worry a lot about that. It's got real people in it, they're right, I know they're right, I can hear them. I hate that precious suburban shit, Updike, Roth, Bellow, all those academic phonies. I don't read much, I don't want to be influenced.

I'm not a very good mixer. Most of the girls are on pills, dope, whatnot. Eight hours a day with men you despise does something to you. I don't even drink, I keep a little ahead that way. The idea is to bust them out, get them to spend their money. A bottle of champagne costs $50, you get $10. My buddy Water Moccasin, she's black, she knows what to say, she gets them going, she'll promise them anything, they bring the bottle of champagne, she has one sip, she's on to the next table. At the end of the nignt they're all waiting around, we slip out the back door. She says Ah know it's bad, Ah know it's wrong, but Ah'm makin $1,400 a week. This one guy, he has handfuls of $100 bills, he was waving them around, he said I was born with a silver spoon in my mouth. Well she said Ah was born with a gold spoon up mah ass. How was that? Not bad huh? She's my lady, she taught me a lot of stuff.

Then there's the Vice Squad, that's a whole other story. They raid the place about once a month, just to keep up appearances. Charles pays off the Sheriff and police. The Mayor wouldn't let us get shut down anyway, we bring the town too much business, all those country boys come to Denver with their oil money to look at the girls.

Water Moccasin got arrested one night because her paste-ups were too small. The areolas aren't supposed to be showing, that's the brown area around the nipples. The guy's young, he's green, he's got black hair and sparkling blue eyes, he's right out of the Marines, he's going to clean up the world. There's a poker game in five figures going at one of the tables, in the next room somebody's hosing a guy down, that's called dirty mixing, like giving a guy a hand job. So he arrests Water Moccasin cause her tits are showing, it was a riot.

118

CIGARETTES

I sat down with these two girls from Connecticut in the Fo'c's'le to bum a cigarette. They bought me a beer too, three, four beers, lota beers. They talked with these tough accents, their lips hardly moved, they were third-grade teachers, I could hardly believe that.

So I took them to the Governor Bradford, I did my usual thing, played pool. They were fighting the whole time, I was right in the middle, trying to keep the peace, trying to get a piece.

So I did my thing, I said you know Come on home and see my etchings. I showed them my stuff, they were very impressed. We sat around and talked, they were looking for a place to stay so I suggested they stay with me, it's a big bed. I wanted one or the other, I would've liked you know both.

They were too straight for that, they had to go to the Holiday Inn. So I followed them out there in my car, I sat around in their room while they argued. They both kept saying You go with him, I'll stay here.

So finally one of them came back to my studio and I fucked her. She kept saying I don't take my pills any more, I broke up with my boyfriend. I said you know I'll pull my dick out before I come, she should've known better, she was a third-grade teacher, I didn't really rape her, I just pushed a little.

Then Wally came in, that's the only time I ever have visitors. I jumped up and put my pants on, she hid under the covers. I said you know Nobody cares. She said I'm embarrassed. So after Wally left, I turned him on, she blew her nose and washed her face and we went back to the Holiday Inn. I kept wondering how I could get the other one but there was no way. They were terrible people anyway, one was completely miserable, I never got to know the other.

So I took them to Piggy's, where else you going to go in Provincetown, I felt obliged to show them around. The place was packed, I just left them at the door, I disappeared, I went and sat with Sally and some people, I lost them for about an hour, I didn't want to be anywhere near them, I felt guilty though, I was afraid they'd be insulted.

All of a sudden the other one popped up. She said I'm desperate, can you help me? I said Certainly. She said Linda's lost, that's the one I fucked, the gloomy one. The music was getting good, I didn't want to leave, we drove all the way back to the Holiday Inn, she wasn't there, she was in Piggy's when we got back. The other one said I hate her, I feel like hitting her.

I said Oh no you came down here together, you've go to stick together. By this time she's rubbing up against me, I didn't want her any more, I was disgusted. So we all wound up at The Hermit, I sat there drinking coffee, I wasn't going to leave. Finally about four they got up, they said how nice it was to meet me, I couldn't believe it. I said Oh before you go can I have a cigarette?

THE BLOND MIDDLE CLASS

Let's just sit here awhile and drink our beer and look at that little lovely, isn't she beautiful, isn't she sweet, wouldn't you love to fuck her? Look at the way her little bottom hits the chair when she sits down, imagine stripping her, think of that cunt, all dewy and new. I'd like to suck some pussy tonight, I've got to be careful, I can't control myself, I'm all ache, it's like the Sistine Chapel, you know the two reaching hands that're just about to touch? God and Man. Michelangelo. There was a guy.

I could've fucked three different chicks last week but I didn't. It wouldn't've been worth it. Maybe it's the weather, they're all in the middle of breaking up with friends of mine. You go to bed with them once, and then they get back together again, and you're an asshole. No thanks.

I've been looking at her trying to find a flaw and I can't, that's a scary edge. I knew guys fell in love, that was the end of them, they never wrote anything. Look at those tits! Think of her tight little squid! Oh Jesus, Lord deliver me, look at her!

I'm having this fantasy, she loves me, her father's got millions, she drives a Jaguar, she's taking me to Jamaica. Never happen. I'd go over but I'm shy. Girls like that take one look at my proletarian mug. What I need is one of those three-day things, and then they go back where they came from and you never see them again.

You ever fuck Ada? Phyllis Phox? I said to her one night at the Reillys I just got a premonition I'm going to fuck you. Well she said If it happens it happens. I like her, she's all right.

You ever fuck a chick in the asshole? Someday I'm going to. These middle-class girls'll do anything, they don't have any inhibitions, my wife never would. I hated that bitch the minute I met her, nine years I lived with her, I never dug her body. I know you're not supposed to make distinctions like that, but I couldn't get into the spiritual shit, tastes differ, she didn't excite me. We had some great fights though.

Last lay I had we were sitting in my bus looking at the ocean, nice moon. She said D'you like bringing strange chicks out here and fucking them? I said Yeah.

Look at her, have you even looked at her? You're in a coma, man. You know some of these longhaired chicks here haven't ever been made love to, I mean really made love to. Like in and out a few times with the fishermen. Wouldn't you love to be the one!

It's been a heavy week. This is in confidence, don't tell anyone. I fucked a nigger in the asshole, I'm not kidding, that's perilous ground, I could see the appeal of it. That's slippery on the soul. I didn't mean nigger. Negro. I always wanted to get a girl that way. I've got to call my mother tonight.

122

HENRY JAMES

Last summer there was this grandmother and her six year old grandson living on airplanes between Amsterdam and New York, they just went back and forth, as soon as the plane refueled they got on again, they never left the airports, I read about it in *The Times*. It was some legal thing about an inheritance, something about international boundaries, she was trying to save his legacy by keeping him aloft. It went on for months, there must've been a fortune involved. The grandmother died, she actually died on one of those flights. I don't know what happened to the kid or his money. Now if it were Henry James sitting here he'd make a notation in his notebook when he got home tonight and someday he'd have himself another story.

123

DISCRIMINATION

I don't believe Barbara Bush, she came over to my house yesterday with all her, what shall I call them? Manuscripts. She said Since I consider you my best friend I want you to read these and tell me what you think of them.

I don't even like Barbara Bush, I literally can't stand her, I have absolutely no use for Barbara Bush but for some reason I couldn't refuse. I don't know what makes her think we're friends, I hardly even know her, she went to bed with Sam Williams one night back when we were living together, the first thing she did was come tell me, I think she likes very involved relationships.

She stayed for three and a half hours, I couldn't get rid of her, I didn't even offer her a cup of tea, not a drop of anything the whole time, that's how rude I was. She just sat there passing me the pages, it was sheer drivel, I began to dread the moment I'd have to say something about it, I knew I'd never have the nerve to tell her it was no good.

Part of it was like a journal, it was very personal. I didn't want to read what Sam Williams meant to her or what she meant to Sam Williams, and I told her so. She said You know it's the kind of thing you scribble when you get home from Piggy's at two in the morning, it's bound to be personal. I said Yes but it's also the sort of thing you put in the trash when you wake up. She wasn't the least bit insulted, she started talking about selling her stories to magazines, then she said But some people like my poems best.

Then she started telling me about this guy she seduced just because she was curious, because he was a challenge, she said he has a reputation for being impossible to make. Little by little it dawned on me that she was talking about the man I've been sleeping with lately. She said he was terrible in bed, she said it was a waste of her time, she said he was no good at all, a complete disappointment. I sat there, I didn't say a word, but right then I decided that's the end for him, he's too undiscriminating.

TAPE RECORDER

A couple we knew, actually we liked them quite a lot, came over to do an article on Dugan for some magazine. The husband took some pictures and used a tape recorder. The interview went off all right, and then we sat down to have lunch. The guy's wife didn't even know what he was doing. We were having dessert and all of a sudden she looked down and said What's that thing going around and around under the table? He said You bastard!

We never felt quite the same about them after that.

THE BRAINLESS BROTHERS

Armand knew they'd never take the bottle back. It was awful slop but they're too stupid to distinguish, he knew exactly what they'd say, they'd say Well we sell a lot of that brand, nobody's ever complained before. Then they'd taste it and say What's wrong with that?

So he poured half the wine out and replaced it with vinegar and took it in and said you know Can I have another bottle, this one's gone bad. And the guy, I don't know which one it was, says That's our most popular brand, no one's ever complained before. And Armand says Well try it and see what you think, he even had a paper cup with him, and wouldn't you know the guy tastes it and says What's wrong with that?

126

ALMOST ALL IN THE FAMILY

He says Help me move this TV. I says Is it hot? No he says. So we were carrying it to the car from the house beside the house he stole it from the night before and we were seen by a woman in the house across the street who knew about the theft and called the police.

So the cops drive up and he says I just shot up on heroin, I don't know what I'm doing. The police said Never mind that, we don't know this is a stolen TV, if you'll just turn it over to us we'll return it to the owner, we won't worry about where it came from.

Oh no he says That's no stolen TV, so they arrested him and they almost arrested me. I think they let me off because I was born here and because he kept saying I was innocent. The cops pride themselves on being hardass, usually they bust everybody they can, all my friends have got time hanging over their heads, or they split and can't come back.

127

A RIBALD CLASSIC

Joe Finch spent a night with Lucy once, but never again. He hounded her constantly but she was in the midst of trying to decide whether to marry Grant. So she went to Aruba for a few days to think it over, where she met the tennis player she married and divorced after marrying and divorcing Grant.

Anyway, when Finch got wind of her trip he said to Sally, his wife You need a vacation, let's go to Aruba. He took a room in Lucy's hotel, flew down the next day, installed Sally and called Lucy from the lobby, who said Come on up.

She gave him the business, induced him to undress, then shoved him out in the hall and locked the door. He banged and whispered and pled and finally she put his clothes outside.

Next day he and Sally are having breakfast, a note slips under their door. Finch beats her to it, he's on his way to the bathroom to tear it up and flush the pieces but she grabs it away from him.

It says Come by again Joe and fuck me the way you did last night.

So it turned into a sort of second honeymoon Finch said. Sally wouldn't let him out unless he fucked her all the time, and they were there for five whole days, heh-heh.

BIG ONE, LITTLE ONE

I saw the most incredible confrontation between two chicks at Ciro's last night, that's the place you go to look at the bartenders, they were having this amazing fight, I couldn't believe the things they were saying to each other. There was a big one and a little one sitting at the end of the bar, I thought I know who's doing all the talking, I was wrong incidentally, when I looked the little one was saying I'd like to push his face in, I'd like to just put my hand on his face and push it in, you oughta push his face in.

The big one kept saying What did he do, tell me what he did, the little one kept saying If a man did that to me I'd push his face in, you don't even know what he did, he degraded you, you didn't even notice.

The guy was sitting at one of the tables looking at them as if he didn't understand one word. I figured out what happened was the little one was walking by their table and saw the guy do something, I never found out what it was, and asked the big one to get up for a minute.

She kept saying I know how you think, I know what you're feeling even if you're too blocked to feel it, you take getting degraded for granted. The big one kept saying I don't want to push his face in, I like him.

It was amazing, I mean this couple was sitting there and this perfect stranger lit into them. It was almost enough to make me want to join Women's Lib, mostly I just wanted to take the poor guy's hand and lead him out of there, he was cute.

129

ARRESTED

I got arrested yesterday. I was going around Ryder Street, Grummit said I was going too fast, I wasn't, then he got me for having New Jersey plates and being a resident, he tried to say the car was mine, it's Gabby's, he said I'm going to impound this car. Do it I said Go ahead I dare you. Whatever you do it better be legal. Out in the light I was okay, I was so mad I wasn't even worried, there were two joints in the car, I just looked at him like he was some kind of asshole.

I said If you're going to arrest me arrest me. You know I've lived in this town five years, I'm a registered voter, I don't want to be treated like a tourist, I used to work for the Highway Department, I always drove with those plates. Grummit says Where you work? I told him the liquor store. He said No you don't, I go in there all the time, I know everyone in there, you don't work there.

So he told me my rights and took me over to the station. I said This is absurd. There were some local guys I knew standing around, they knew it was all bullshit, they just sort of moved away, like they weren't even watching. A police-girl told me my rights again, and then this guy at the desk says, he holds up my license and he says Let's get this straight. I said You just told me anything I say can be used against me, I'm not saying a word, I want to talk to my lawyer. Grummit spreadeagled me up against the wall and searched me and took my wallet and belt. I was in jail four hours, made me paranoid, freaked me right out, I'm down in this dungeon. They let me make a phone call afterwards.

The bondsman didn't need any money because he knew me. It's harrassment, that's all it is.

Grummit brought in another guy for not seeing him and not stopping right away and put him in a cell. He leaned up against the bars and said Well Buster who d'you think's smarter now? It's a good thing you stopped when you did, I'd've put one of these right through the windshield, and he patted his holster.

ME TOO

He stopped me too. I was on my way to unemployment. He was just waiting there stopping people evidently. He said I was going too fast, I was going regular town speed, 20-25 at most. He was looking at my license and registration when this TV repair truck went by, it really was going fast. Grummit yelled at him and he stopped. It was a young guy, long hair, hippie type, he got out and began to give Grummit all kinds of shit, he shouted You've got to prove it. He was right but man. Grummit handed me back my license and said That's okay, you can go, I've got a better one.

SURPRISE, SURPRISE

It's like being in love
with a mousetrap. She says
Come here little mouse, I'm
not really a mousetrap, I
won't hurt you, SNAP. Oh
poor little mouse,
did I hurt you?
I didn't mean to hurt
you, poor little mouse,
come here.

132

MANIAC

When Harold was living with me I woke up one night and someone was beating my head against the wall. I watched it happen, I didn't say a word, I watched this head being rammed into the wall like a post, and it was me. I had this amazing detachment, I wanted to see who this maniac was so I put on the light. Oh it's you Harold I said. I could see he was angry. I went into this whole reasonable rap. I said You're Harold, I'm me, if my body belongs to you then you've got two and I don't have any, that's not fair. Well he said I'm mad. I really blew up. I said Get out of my bed, get out of my house, get out of my life, goodbye. By this time he was standing by the bed with this confused look on his face. He got dressed and then he got undressed and got back in bed and he said I don't have anyplace to go at this time of night. He went right back to sleep but I stayed awake all night waiting for this maniac to attack me again. I kept saying to myself You fool, you fool. I don't know what he was so mad about but that was approximately when he moved out.

HEADFUCK

Harold came over this morning and he said I just wanted to let you know where we stand, we're through, you're not going to be the woman in my life, I'd like you to be but you're not, I need a woman in my life and I'm going out to find her right now. I said I don't want to be the woman in your life, I never wanted to be the woman in your life, put an ad in *The Advocate*, though it doesn't come out till Thursday. He said You don't want me but you don't want to let me go. So we sat down and had some coffee and he said I've decided what you're best at is freaking people out. I said Well are we square now? No he said As a matter of fact you owe me five dollars from that bet. I said You petty fuck and I threw it at him and he ripped it up and then I went him one better and burned it. He said Don't worry you'll still get your birthday present. I said I don't want any birthday present, just go.

He called me about noon, he said You know I didn't mean any of those things I said. I said I don't believe anything you say.

134

NIGHTWORK

Henry had left him after six years, simply moved out and cancelled their life together. Arthur had been the one who always felt confined, threatening to leave, lamenting his lost freedom. Now he was in despair and looked a ghost.

"Don't do anything reckless, that's the coward's way," Henry said, fear in his voice, when they parted after an accidental encounter on the street.

Arthur went back to his empty apartment, swallowed 30 relaxer pills, wrote a note saying, "I took the coward's way," left it on the stairs outside and went to bed. He lay on his back, eyes wide open, energy surging through every nerve. At 10 P.M. Carol found the note and drove him to the Drop-in Center.

He felt increasingly exhilarated and embarrassed. "I got them from a doctor in Boston," he told Sara, who couldn't find the pill in the *Physician's Desk Reference*. "They were supposed to help me relax, I'm a very tense person."

She gave him an Ipecac to make him vomit, but he only belched.

"Try putting your finger down your throat," she said.

"I've never been able to do that," he said, "I can drink this stuff, but I can't do that."

She gave him another Ipecac and he drank two more glasses of water, while the fumes fouled the air. "I'm awfully sorry," he said, "I can't seem to."

"Maybe you're too relaxed," she said. "How do you feel?"

"Actually in some weird way never better," he said. He felt like he had taken some terrific kind of speed that made sensations race and time stop simultaneously. Each object looked uniquely, hypnotically, bright and clear, even the bare corners and cracked walls. He felt the possibilities of perfect happiness, a need for nothing but life itself, pure sensate interest.

Sara was scared. His eyes and vital signs were normal, but 30 of anything is a lot, so she called Dr. Farlow, who came in ten minutes, delicately drunk and steady.

"You'd better keep him overnight," he said. "You might have to walk him around and give him coffee, don't let him go to sleep, check his blood pressure once in a while."

"I don't want to keep him here," Sara said. "The hospital's an hour and a half away."

"An hour," Dr. Farlow murmured. "He'll be all right."

"I really feel he ought to go to the hospital," Sara said.

"It's not necessary," Dr. Farlow said in a steely tone without moving his lips or taking his eyes off Arthur. "I'm not going to authorize an ambulance for this."

"I really think you ought to go to the hospital," she said to Arthur. "Something might go wrong."

"*Then* you can call the Rescue Squad," Dr. Farlow said.

"I could drive him up right now," Carol said.

"Great!" Sara said, sagging with relief.

Dr. Farlow gave them all a look of indignant contempt, picked up his bag and departed in silence.

"Oh God, must I really go to the hospital?" Arthur said. "This is mortifying, I do apologize to you all."

"Come on, Arthur," Carol said. "It'll be a nice ride, it's almost a full moon."

After an hour on the road he grew silent. "Are you all right?" she said.

"Yes," he said, but slumped against the door.

She drove the rest of the way at 80, taking one hand off the wheel to shake him, shouting and shouting, but got no response.

From the emergency entrance he was rushed to intensive care, pumped out and broken from his coma.

The Drop-in Center is closed from midnight till 8 am. About 11:55 a boy came in, held out his palm with a blue pill in it and said, "I just took a whole bunch of these that I just found in this coat that I borrowed, what are they?"

Sara found them in the *P.D.R.* but wasn't sure whether he was disappointed or glad when she told him they were harmless. He thanked her and left and she put out the perpetual TV watchers—The Stinker, The Boy Bum, The Improbable Prostitute, as she had come to dub them, her initial sympathy waned. These three especially seemed to have embraced their fate, though all were dour,resentful and surly. The Stinker had a sarcastic tongue for those who, innocently entering his aura, recoiled visibly; The Boy Bum had an unnerving shamble and mature vices; and the girl kept her appearance such that no one would have paid her much.

The bars close at one. Too keyed up to sleep Sara lay on her back listening to the raucous crowd spilling in the street. It had an ominous gibbering sound, as of voices on the edge of control, and after a little arpeggio of shrieks and cries her dread materialized in a sudden thudding of feet on the porch and the loudly-ringing bell. She jumped up and unlocked the door and the Rescue Squad brought in unconscious and laid on the couch a tall tanned handsome blond longhaired boy with a bloody face. He had on a SuperStar T-shirt, a big silver belt buckle and studded boots, and he breathed in and out evenly as if asleep. Sara couldn't get his eyes to dilate. Dr. Farlow arrived a minute later.

The Rescue Squad guessed he'd been rolled, because of the gash in his head and his lack of a wallet. They had found him staggering in the A-House Alley. He had said his name was Jim before collapsing.

Dr. Farlow bandaged the gash, checked his signs, and looked in his eyes with a light.

"I can't get them to dilate," Sara said.

"Yes, they're all right," he said. He slapped the boy's face back and forth. "Jim, Jim," he called. "Wake up, Jim."

Jim tried to ward off the blows by scrunching his face and rolling half over, but Farlow pulled him back and slapped him. "Come on, Jim, wake up."

Jim made an extended intricate sound as if answering with his mouth closed, a defiant complaint, followed by a sigh of comfort.

"He'll sleep it off," Farlow said.

"I'm very worried about that head wound," Sara said. "He doesn't respond much."

Farlow tapped Jim's knee with a percussion hammer, then examined his eyes again. "He's a little slow, he'll be all right, he's on something or drunk."

Sara was afraid he ought to go to the hospital but didn't dare oppose the doctor again. The Rescue Squad, bunched in the doorway, looked down impassively at SuperStar, waiting for the word — to make the trip to Hyannis, or go back to bed.

With a negligent gesture Dr. Farlow dismissed them and went home to his bottle. Sara unhappily locked the door again, put a pillow under Jim's head and a blanket over him, and went to bed on the other couch.

The street noise hardly ceased the whole hot night while she braced for the next knock, and at dawn, just as she was finally sinking into an exhausted doze, the boy started to choke.

She sprang up, turned his mouth to one side and a bloodclot like a beet slopped in her lap. He couldn't get his breath and shook like death throes.

She called Dr. Farlow who came instantly — as if he'd never gone to bed — and examined Jim's eyes. "They weren't like this before," he said, panic behind his voice, but Sara was too angry to answer.

The ambulance pulled up outside. Farlow still couldn't get a response from the boy though his breathing had cleared and he moaned deep in his sleep. They loaded him in and hooked up the oxygen.

"What do these guys do to themselves?" the driver said in amazed disgust, and the orange and white van with flashing lights accelerated silently through the dreaming town.

Jim was unconscious for two days and the drug was never identified but a week later Sara saw him in a bright new SuperStar T-shirt sitting surrounded by girls on the steps of The Green Lantern, watching the action across the street at the Spiritus Pizza. He had a jaunty Band-Aid over one eye and looked regal with the sun in his hair and his court of chicks.

The Drop-in Center reopens at 8. Sara locked the door again, wiped some of the blood off her, lay down and the phone rang. The caller said a man was having a fit on the street, just half a block away, and maybe the Rescue Squad should be sent. When Sara asked for details the caller returned from her window to say the victim had disappeared. "I'll go out and look," Sara said, opened the door and found Bob Brownley on the stoop.

He was in his work clothes, teeth chattering, face wet with sweat, eyes terrified.

"Why didn't you knock?" she said.

"I can wait till you open," he said.

She helped him inside and steered him to the clean couch, got him laid down with a blanket over him. He kept sitting up and glaring, and his clothes danced on him.

"When was the last time you had a drink?"

"Three days ago," he said. "This just came on."

"Is there anything I can do, do you want some water?" she said.

"No, I'll just have to sweat it out," he said.

"If you don't stop drinking you'll kill yourself one of these times," she said.

"I know it," he said.

EITHER/OR

Sometimes I see the advantages. One night I was in Piggy's, George and Philip were both there, both giving me a hard time. I kept trying to keep away from them, it was like being in a vice, I kept moving around and one or the other would keep popping up, demanding I go home with him. I just wanted to be left alone.

Royal could see my troubles, he came over and stood beside me. He puts his cheek right close to mine, he says When that happens to me darling I just wait till closing time and then leave with a man.

SOUVENIRS

That's the way it is in this town, there's always a connection. Somebody introduced me to him at Ciro's one night, we got into a heavy rap right away. He's very intense, very serious. I was going through a bad time and I needed a lot of small talk, I didn't feel like going to bed with anybody. We talked on the telephone four or five times after that and he asked me to dinner one night, so I went.

I think I must have talked more than I ordinarily would because he was a stranger, it was one of the worst times of my life, I was drinking myself silly from about noon every day, I never knew where I was going to wake up or where the car would be, I broke three fingers and never knew how, it was obvious I was out to do myself in. All my dreams were about killing people, I hated all my friends, I was just filled with anger and frustration. I was so desperate I was going to go home for a while.

He got very angry, he said You don't know what anger is, and he jumped up and tore off my sneakers and threw them through the window. It's his mother's house, there's all this china. I ran out the door, I didn't stop to pick them up.

He called me the next day. I said I don't particularly want to see you again, I can't handle that kind of behavior.

Next time I saw him was in Ciro's again, it was months later. I was sitting with some people, when he saw me he just stared, he said What're you doing here again? I think he was indignant to find me in a bar. Jack Watson said Why shouldn't she be here, she can be anywhere she wants. That was very sweet of him. I said I live here.

He sat down and began to talk, he had this terrible hunger and loneliness, you know how it is when somebody fixes on you like you're their sole hope. He's almost a hermit, he said he only goes out to look for girls. He's very angry and he knows it, he does hard physical labor to let it off, like he chops down a forest a day or something. He's a disappointed man, he wrote a book and it was rejected, I guess it was a kind of wisdom book, and now he says the ideas of the drug culture have superceded it. It's like he had a dream for us, all of us, and we failed to fulfill it.

At closing time he said I'll walk you home, so I invited him in. As soon as he got in my house he took off his shoes and began to prowl around looking at everything, which made me bristle of course. I said How do you expect to change the world when you never make contact with people? Where do you get off blaming people when your dreams don't come true? I said You're wasting your life. He said Maybe you're right, but where does that leave me?

Fortunately the phone rang. It was Royal, he says Come on over here and be with all the straight people you invited. I'd forgotten all about this party. The last one of his was 95% gay, I get tired of being a fag-hag, so I invited everyone I ran into. When we got there he took one look and left. I haven't seen him since, I guess he's still in town.

At one time, like six years ago, he was in love with a girl named Moment who's not here any more, she's back in Boston with a Klee print of mine on her wall. She was a very spacy chick, she was always on something, she gave him a hard time, going to bed with everybody. He loaned her his car, she was moving from one place to another, she never came back, she met some friends with acid and left the car at Race Point, he didn't find it for a week.

I was living at Number 28 alone. I had a party one night and Sam Williams came with Emma Broad, I'd never met him before. The next night I came in and found him asleep on my couch, she'd kicked him out. He said Can I stay here until I find a place? Three months later we're still living together.

I had to go back to New York, I was making good money, I paid the rent on the place and came up weekends. I began to sense somebody else was living there, they did a good job of covering up. I didn't say anything, I was afraid of losing him. It turned out to be Moment. I confronted him with it one time, he burst into tears and promised he was never going to have anything more to do with her, she was probably driving him crazy by that time. I guess when she leaves she always takes something. Another mutual friend was in her new apartment recently and noticed my Klee, not to mention his own cappuccino maker. She was more their type, they wanted me to talk to.

THE SENSIBLE THING

They should all be shot. They'd be waked up early some cold misty morning lying there in the Lincoln bedroom, they wouldn't even have time to brush their teeth. Come along now, you'll have to come. They'd walk out under the dripping trees, the grass would get their slippers wet. The Cabinet and their wives and children would already be there in their bathrobes, they hadn't expected it to turn out this way. There'd be these soldiers in anonymous clothes standing around with guns. The bulldozers would've been going all night digging this big ditch. No last words, just plow them in and cover them over. Then we wouldn't have to put up with any more of this shit.

THE ULTIMATE QUESTION

I'm leaving.
I know I say it
all the time but
I'm going away
one of these days, make
the big break, move
to New York, L.A.,
Shanghai. I'm getting my shit
together, I'm really going
to do it, you'll see, you'll be
amazed, you'll get a card
from Tulsa or Toledo
or some other slum
and you'll remember
what I said tonight
when you thought I was drunk.
By then I'll be long gone,
free and clear. Of course
I've only been here 17 years.
You can't stay forever
can you?

The Apple-wood Press began in January 1976. The image of the apple joined with the hard concreteness of wood in many ways expresses the goals of the press. One of the first woods used in printing, apple-wood remains a metaphor for giving ideas a form. Apple-wood Press books are published in the memory of Harry and Lillian Apple.